'Tangles in my ... she told him. ' ... life I've doubts** ...

'Me too,' he murmured, but he kissed her anyway, right on the back of her neck where the already sensitised skin burned to his touch.

She turned into his arms, felt him reach out to turn off the gas, then met his lips in a kiss that had been so long anticipated she shuddered with the relief of it.

'I don't want to get involved,' he reminded her breathlessly, a little later.

She kissed the words away, although when once again the exploration left lips to savour skin she did manage a slightly shaky, 'Nor do I.'

Meredith Webber says of herself, 'Previously a teacher, shopkeeper, travel agent, pig farmer, builder and worker in the disability field (among other things), the 'writing bug' struck me unexpectedly. I entered a competition run by a women's magazine, shared the third prize with two hundred and fifty other would-be writers, and found myself infected. Thirty-something books later, I'm still suffering. Medical romances appeal to me because they offer the opportunity to include a wider cast of characters, and the challenge of interweaving a love story into the drama of medical or paramedical practice.'

Recent titles by the same author:

A VERY PRECIOUS GIFT
REDEEMING DR HAMMOND
CLAIMED: ONE WIFE
FOUND: ONE HUSBAND

THE TEMPTATION TEST

BY
MEREDITH WEBBER

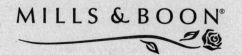

MILLS & BOON®

MILLS & BOON and MILLS & BOON with the Rose Device are registered trademarks of the publisher.

First published in Great Britain 2001
Harlequin Mills & Boon Limited,
Eton House, 18-24 Paradise Road, Richmond, Surrey TW9 1SR

© Meredith Webber 2001

ISBN 0 263 82705 4

Set in Times Roman 10 on 10½ pt.
03-1201-56372

Printed and bound in Spain
by Litografia Rosés, S.A., Barcelona

CHAPTER ONE

NOAH BLACKLOCK was cursing all women as he drove along the narrow, deeply rutted sand track from his bush retreat towards the main road to town. Quite how he could pin his lateness this particular morning on the universal female conspiracy to drive him completely insane he wasn't sure, but he knew it had to be a woman's doing.

The powerful Jeep engine growled in low gear as it churned the wheels through the soft sand. Not far now! Around the bend, down the hill, and he'd be on the gravel road to town—the main highway only a few hundred metres beyond the little settlement. He'd make that appointment yet.

He took the bend too fast, and the Jeep slid sideways before the tyres gripped again and he regained control.

Then slammed on the brakes as the rear of an old Toyota LandCruiser came closer…and closer…and—

The Jeep stopped inches from the obstruction, and Noah leapt out, a mouthful of colourful words ready for the driver stupid enough to stop on the blind corner.

A woman, of course!

And blonde as well.

One of those curvy, long-legged, white-blonde blondes—the prototype for blonde jokes.

She was standing, jack in one hand and a metal stabilising plate in the other, staring at the sand-encrusted front nearside tyre on her wreck of a vehicle.

He bit back the words he wanted to yell at her, grabbed the plate and the jack, slid them into place beneath the front chassis and was about to lift the front of the vehicle when he remembered the first rule of tyre-changing. Loosen the nuts while the wheel's on the ground.

He'd noticed the tool kit lying on the sand.

'I—' she began, in a soft, slightly husky voice.

5

'Just don't talk. Don't say a word!' he growled at this latest member of the female species fate had flung in his path to anger and frustrate him. His body might be registering the flowery perfume she was wearing, but recent events meant his brain was very much in control.

'But—'

He held up his hand to cut off her protest, and scowled another warning at her, then grabbed the wheel brace and began to loosen the nuts. The cause of this morning's problems stepped back, as if to admire his skill, and folded her arms beneath breasts he couldn't help but notice. The male ego he tried to control immediately went into show-off mode, increasing the speed with which he worked.

He jacked up the car, whipped off the nuts, wrestled the wheel from the spokes and turned to the woman.

'Where's your spare?'

She smiled at him, and he realised she was more than just a woman, she was a beautiful woman.

Not that he would allow such an incidental observation to distract him.

'Well?'

The smile grew wider, showing even white teeth. It glimmered in eyes as blue as the evening sky, and pressed a dimple deep into her right cheek.

'That's it.' She pointed a slim, pink-tipped finger towards the tyre he held balanced between his hands.

'You mean you haven't got a decent tyre to replace this one?' The anger he'd held in check earlier came roaring forth, like flames from a flamethrower. 'And you're out here, alone, on an isolated road? Women!'

He flung up his arms in disgust and the tyre fell over, clipping his shin and sending him off balance so he stumbled and had to reach out for support.

The woman's hand caught his arm and steadied him, but the noises coming from her were more like chuckles of delight than soothing murmurs or placating apologies.

'That is the spare,' she managed to gasp between gales of unseemly laughter. 'The flat one's in the back. I'd just finished changing it when you came along and, being a man, you had to charge in and do your macho thing!'

'Why didn't you stop me? Tell me?' He knew he was yelling because his voice was echoing back to him from the sandhills over by the lake.

She stepped away from him and shrugged, the movement lifting her breasts so he was torn between wanting to kill her and an urge to get a better look at the soft protuberances.

'After you'd told me to shut up? And scowled so ferociously I was all aquiver? A poor defenceless woman like myself all alone out here in the bush?'

Strangling would be good. He'd take his time about it! Have her begging…

'Well, are you going to put it back on for me so I can get to work, or do I have to do it myself?'

He reined in wayward thoughts of the beauty begging for something very different to murder and tried to concentrate on the current situation.

'Put it back on?' he muttered, wondering what on earth they'd been talking about.

'The tyre,' she said helpfully. 'Now I've done a practice run I'll even give you a hand.'

She bent over, tipped the tyre up on its tread and proceeded to roll it towards the car. By the time she was ready to lift it onto the wheel studs, he realised he should be helping, not watching the length of leg revealed by her bending over in a very short skirt.

'Let me!' he grumbled, taking command again—of the tyre and hopefully his thoughts.

He heaved the heavy beast up and turned it until he could slide it into place, aware that the woman was taking some of the weight—but more aware of her as a woman.

It's a woman who got you stuck out here in the first place, mate, his head reminded his rebellious body. A blonde, remember?

He picked up the nuts and began to fit them.

'You must be lost if you're on this road,' he said, aiming for a little normality in this bizarre situation.

'No. I'm staying down there a little way,' she said, waving her hand towards the track down which he'd just travelled.

'Exactly where down there?' he demanded. There was nowhere 'down there' but his place.

She passed him the wheel brace.

'Suspicious cuss, aren't you?' she teased, blue eyes again alight with laughter. 'At Matt Ryan's place, if you must know.'

Now disappointment warred with disbelief. He went with the second reaction as the first didn't bear thinking about.

'The old Ryan place? It's falling down. What's happened? Matt gone feral, has he? Decided to give up the high life and start living the way he pretends to in his documentaries? I can just see that!'

The cutting edge of sarcasm forced Jena to defend her employer.

'Matt lives those documentaries! He takes on those challenges!'

'Yeah, right!' the stranger growled, releasing the pressure on the jack so the tyre slapped back onto the ground with a jolting thud. 'Him and his make-up person, and his hairstylist—not to mention a ten-man support crew. Some challenge!'

He was mocking her dream to be the first woman to take on the type of adventure challenges Matt faced, and Jena, who'd already had a particularly tiresome morning, felt the heat of anger burning in her chest.

'He travels alone on his challenges. OK, there's a camera crew but they're not with him in his vehicle, and the rest of the crew go on ahead—'

'To erect the tents, set up his comfortable bed, cook his meal, cool his wine. Wave the bloody fans above his perspiring head, most probably! Yes, ma'am! That's a real challenge!'

'Well, it is,' she fumed, snatching the jack out of his hand and storming to the back of the vehicle to fling it in. 'And his documentaries are sold worldwide, watched by millions of people—'

'Who all end up with the misguided idea that life in

Australia is one long bout of wrestling crocodiles, trekking through snake-infested jungles or clinging precariously to precipitous rocks. The man stages his challenges then acts like a hero for carrying them out.'

He paused for breath and Jena, who should have interrupted at that stage, found herself admiring how his chest expanded as it filled with air. He was a tall, solid man, well put together. Dark haired, and with the kind of craggy face which shouldn't have been handsome but was. She realised she'd missed her opportunity when his harangue continued.

'Finding a cure for cancer—that's a challenge. Fixing the problems of homeless youth! Even learning to live on the same planet as women! Take your choice, but let's not get too carried away about Matt bloody Ryan's television show. That's entertainment, Blondie, not a challenge!'

'Don't call me Blondie!' Shamed by her inattention earlier, she snapped the words at him then regretted her outburst when she caught a gleam of satisfaction in his pale eyes.

Grey or pale green?

Unusual whichever they were. With a glint like the sheen of highly polished metal—

'imagine what Matt's doing out at the old place.'

'What Matt's doing there?' she said, frowning at him as she tried to recall the words she'd missed while debating his eye colour. 'Why would Matt be there?'

The eyes—grey, she decided—scanned down her body, then back up again, answering her question with silent insolence.

Jena clenched her hands into fists to stop herself hitting him.

She spun away before the temptation proved too great. Being late for work on the first day of her own personal 'challenge' was hardly the way to prove herself to Matt.

'If he's not there, who's with you?'

The stranger had followed her and reached out to hold the door open as she clambered up into the driver's seat, regretting her decision to cling to her normal 'work' clothes as the skirt rode up to reveal even more leg than usual.

'No one! I'm staying there on my own.' Dumb, dumb,

dumb! 'Of course, I'll have friends coming out. Visiting. Staying over.'

'Of course,' he agreed smoothly. 'No doubt any number of people all dying to keep you company in a ruin of a shack on the edge of nowhere. As my grandmother would say, I'm not as green as I'm cabbage-looking, Blondie.'

She was going to protest about the name again when he leaned across her, peering into the cab.

'I assume you have a mobile. Here, I'll give you my number. Although you can't see my place from where you are it's only about a hundred yards away. If you need anything…'

He drew back and she took a breath, though why a stranger leaning close to her should affect her breathing, she had no idea.

Perhaps because he *was* a stranger!

He handed her a card and she held the stiff white rectangle between her fingers and squinted at the black marks. She'd have given her second-best pair of shoes to know his name but no way was she going to reach over for her handbag and scrabble through it for her reading glasses.

'Do you know the emergency services number?' he continued in his overbearing way. 'It might be a good idea to phone the exchange and get the local police station number as well. Let someone know you're staying out there. The lads in town would love an opportunity to rescue a damsel in distress. Or even check on you occasionally.'

Again his gaze did its scanning thing, but before she could protest he'd shut the door and walked away, leaving Jena with an uneasy feeling in the pit of her stomach.

Murderers don't suggest you check in with the local cops, she told herself as she drove off.

The uneasiness persisted.

More to do with the man than being murdered?

OK, he'd been arresting, in a dark, saturnine kind of way. Not cabbage-looking at all, in fact. But she'd been in the company of attractive men so often that good looks no longer impressed her. It was the inner man that counted—and, as far as she could tell, the stranger's inner man was a dark and angry being.

Not attractive at all.

Noah memorised the number plate as he followed the LandCruiser down the track. What was Matt thinking to let a woman like that—any woman, in fact—stay out at his tumble-down old shack on her own? The place had no power, no phone and probably no water, if the rust holes he'd seen in the tank last time he'd walked past were any indication.

Not that it was any of his business, he reminded himself. In fact, the policy he'd adopted in his childhood to keep out of Matt Ryan's way still held. It had been bad enough having Matt held up to him as the ideal of boyhood all through his youth, but these days Noah's mother spoke Matt's name with something approaching awe—obviously more impressed by television stars than hard-working doctors.

Then there was his determination to avoid all women for a considerable period of time. Especially blondes, given the di-sastrous way they'd featured in his life lately—like some re-curring nightmare—and even more especially, one of Matt Ryan's blondes!

He had avoided Matt assiduously for years, but no one could have avoided hearing of his exploits. The man got better press coverage than all but the most vital of sports games, more publicity than the entire government. And rarely did he appear, in the press or on TV, without a blonde draped across him like a fashion accessory.

According to the tabloids, they were bimbos, every one of them.

Airheads.

Actually, when you considered it, nature might have got it right. Having endowed the woman like the one driving stead-fastly down the road in front of him with more than her share of physical beauty, adding brains would have been overkill.

Sexist! his better self muttered, while his more basic side remembered the length of leg Blondie had revealed as she'd stepped up into the cab of the decrepit old vehicle.

And the flash of anger in her eyes as she'd reacted to the name.

Hmm, his baser self whispered. Might be fun having one of Matt's blondes as a neighbour for a while. Hadn't Matt stolen Bridget Somerton from him? Back when they were teenagers and the surge of adolescent testosterone had combined with long summer days and hot summer nights to make the group who'd holidayed at the lake as randy as young stallions.

No way! he told himself.

No women!

And especially, no blondes.

If this time apart didn't resolve things between Lucy and himself, then when he was ready for another close relationship—which might not be for twenty or so years—he would choose a cool brunette. A career woman. Possibly a lawyer— or perhaps a business executive.

Nuclear physicist? the base self mocked, flashing images of the leggy blonde on an inner screen in his brain.

Jena drove slowly past the shop and three houses which made up the closest habitation to Matt's old shack, then accelerated when she reached the highway. Hard to believe a place as seemingly isolated as Lake Caratha was only fifteen minutes' drive from a bustling town. Kareela served as a regional centre for the tourist areas along the coast, as well as the thriving market gardens which covered the fertile, gently rolling hills behind the coastal strip.

She lifted one hand from the steering wheel to press it against the nerves fluttering in her stomach. Stupid to be nervous. She'd worked as an assistant on similar productions to this, been the general dogsbody who'd caught the blame for everything that had gone wrong, from the star being sick to an untimely thunderstorm. Being a liaison person should be a piece of cake.

Maybe the flutters were a reaction to the angry man. She grinned to herself. Tall, dark and angry: a perfect description of him. Although the more usual 'handsome' would also have fitted—if you liked looks which went beyond the conventional standards of good looks. She slowed as she entered the town's lower speed zone.

The hospital was on a hill overlooking the town—third turn on the left if the map she had was accurate.

She looked around her with interest, not having seen much the previous day when she'd driven through. It was less than a month until Christmas, and the local council had already begun to install street decorations. Pregnant-bellied bells were tied to lampposts and workers were stringing coloured lights across the street.

By Christmas she'd be out of here—hopefully, with a guarantee from Matt that she'd be part of the new challenge series he was planning.

Though she'd have to succeed with the job at the hospital, as well as stick out the three weeks in his terrible old shack.

Before making the turn, she glanced in her rear-view mirror and saw the Jeep, its indicator light blinking as if he intended following her.

So he could yell at her again?

She battled the heavy steering, negotiating the turn and heading up the hill.

If he called her Blondie again, she'd yell a little herself. In fact, yelling at him might be good. It might release a little of the tension she was feeling over this job.

Another glance in the rear-view mirror again, and she realised there'd be no yelling by or at anyone. The Jeep had disappeared. Presumably down one of the side streets—although he'd appeared so suddenly he might have the ability to materialise and dematerialise.

She drew into the hospital parking lot and stopped, her eyes taking in the gracious old building. It was a solid brick and stone structure, rising two storeys in its central core, but with the lower storey spread wider, like a skirt, around it.

A shiver of what could have been either excitement or apprehension skittered through her, but she decided not to analyse it. Better to spend the time tidying her hair.

*   *   *

'Is he here yet?' Noah asked as he stalked through the big room which housed a receptionist and the hospital's two general office staff.

Peta Clarke, the more senior of the two secretaries, shook her head.

'Mr Finch's in, though, if you want to see him.'

Noah resisted the impulse to roll his eyes. No sense in embroiling the secretarial staff in personal battles. He should probably be trying to appease the hospital's chief executive officer rather than fighting with him, but the man had no guts—no willingness to go beyond the bounds and try something new, even if it wasn't in the 'how to run a hospital' manual.

It was frustration that was making him angry—first the delay in getting the kids settled in their house, then Jeff Finch's insistence that any plan must be submitted to the Health Department for approval, following 'correct procedure'.

He opened the door to his office, then turned back to have another look at the three women.

Grinned at them.

'Sunday best, although this is only the preliminary skirmish?'

Peta chuckled, and dusted an imaginary thread off her navy skirt.

'Stupid, isn't it? I mean, we've already been told filming won't start for another week, but here we are, all dolled up to the nines.' She grinned as she waved a hand towards her colleagues. 'We've already had a laugh about it.'

Noah returned her smile, and felt slightly better for the moment's amusement, although he doubted whether there'd be much to amuse him during the next few weeks. The first thing he'd have to do would be to explain to this liaison person that Kareela was still a working hospital and no way would he tolerate any interruption to patient services or interference in the staff's performance of their duties. He'd lay down some ground rules.

He checked his watch. And if the man wasn't on time, he'd do a ward round. That'd show him!

The phone buzzed as he was justifying this decision to himself. Patsy, the receptionist, advised him that the representative of the production company was here.

'Have Peta show him in,' he said, deciding it might be advantageous to be sitting behind his desk, looking desperately busy, so that this liaison fellow would know from the beginning that Noah had no time to waste on frivolities.

He settled into his worn leather chair, put on his glasses and pulled a pile of papers towards him. Looking busy wasn't hard for a man who hated paperwork as much as he did.

He heard the door open, then Peta's voice murmuring a name and the door closing again. Judging that his pretence had gone on long enough, he sighed and raised his head, reaching up to remove his reading glasses as he did so.

The image was blurred, but readily identifiable, though the cascade of silvery hair was now swept up on top of her head in some kind of simple but very elegant knot.

'Blondie? What the hell do you want? Going to sue me for changing your car tyre?'

One wing of the glasses hooked behind his ear, so he was now peering lopsidedly in her direction and trying to maintain a modicum of aplomb while feeling like a total idiot.

Which didn't faze his visitor one jot! She stepped calmly forward, held out her hand, and said, 'Perhaps we should have introduced ourselves earlier. I'm Jena Carpenter, liaison person for Showcase Productions.'

She paused and he managed to detach the glasses from his ear. He stretched out his own hand and somehow sent the pile of papers he'd pulled forward sliding across the desk and cascading in a flurry of white towards the floor.

He bent to retrieve them, but Blondie's voice pulled him upright again.

'And you may call me, Jena, or Miss Carpenter, or even "hey, you",' she added, taking the hand which now hovered uncertainly above the desk and allowing a very perfunctory skin contact between their fingers before dropping it cold. 'But if you call me Blondie again I'll sue you for workplace harassment.'

The steely resolution in her indigo eyes told him she meant precisely what she'd said, and he found himself looking away, peering at his hand as if the cool, slim fingers might have stung him.

He looked up at her again.

'Matt Ryan's idea, I assume?' he muttered. 'Did he really think sending a good-looking woman would magically smooth the way for his underlings to do exactly as they please in my hospital?'

'*Your* hospital?' Blondie murmured. What had she said her name was—Jena?

'I'm the senior medical officer,' Noah growled, 'and the patients' comfort and general well-being are my responsibility. *And* my primary concern. I thought I'd explained all this to the first underling Matt sent along.'

Jena took a deep breath, then mentally squared up to the man she was supposed to be appeasing.

'Let's begin again, shall we?' she suggested. 'To start with, although Showcase Productions is a division of the company owned by Matt and his associates, he has no day-to-day control over the running of it, nor does he interfere in the production of the Showcase television programmes. He had nothing to do with the choice of Kareela as a location, or with my appointment as liaison person.'

She wasn't entirely sure the last statement was true and could see the doctor's disbelief in his face, even before he countered with, 'And you staying out at his old place is pure coincidence?'

'Me staying out at his place has nothing to do with this production,' Jena retorted. Which was the truth as far as it went. Though the necessity of living in or near the town for the three weeks had provided her with a fortuitous opportunity to prove a point to Matt.

Her thoughts were brought up short by a scoffing laugh, and a derisive, 'I bet!'

Jena scowled at him.

'Where I live is none of your business, Dr Blacklock,' she snapped. 'So do you think we could get past it, and whatever old history you have with Matt Ryan which makes you so defensive, and discuss the filming?'

He returned her scowl, but added more ferocity, while Jena debated whether Matt *had* influenced the decision to appoint her as liaison. If so, the idea had backfired spectacularly.

Thinking of this reminded her why a liaison person had been appointed. She could score a point here.

'Particularly as it was you who insisted on having one person to deal with throughout the filming,' she added. 'I was appointed because I was the only person within the company who had both production and nursing experience.'

'You're a nurse?'

Noah regretted the words the instant they were out of his mouth, but the blonde—Jena—must have heard such incredulity before. She shrugged her dismissal of the words.

'If you'd read the information package we sent you some weeks ago, you'd know I'm not a nurse but did two years nursing studies with some practical work, which at least qualifies me to tell a bedpan from a thermometer. And as my job here doesn't entail actual nursing, my level of experience isn't important. I think the first priority is to lay down some ground rules.'

He frowned at her, irrationally irritated because she'd used the expression first. He should have said 'Exactly!' and launched into his prepared speech, but she sat down at that moment and her skirt slid up, revealing a not unseemly amount of lightly tanned thigh, enough to make him wonder how celibates managed their libidos.

He also wondered where in the muddle of papers on his desk—and on the floor—the information package was. As she'd said, there'd be background information on her in it somewhere, and it would be interesting...

'I understand that this is a working hospital and although emergency cases are transferred to Brisbane, you still have patients requiring ongoing care. That's why Kareela was chosen. Showcase specialises in ''real-life'' television which is very popular at the moment. I'm here to see the film crew causes the least possible disruption to the running of the hospital.'

Noah again refrained from rolling his eyes, but when his gaze wandered back towards the legs he was distracted.

'Fat chance!' he muttered, then shook his head and reminded himself of his sister's favourite warning—a closed mouth gathers no foot!

Maybe Blondie hadn't heard…

From the fine pleating of her brow, he saw she had.

'You can either help us be as unobtrusive as possible, Dr Blacklock, or you can hinder the process by being obstructive. I understand you didn't want the documentary filmed here, but were won over by an increase in the financial inducement.'

She paused and looked him straight in the eye.

'We're not only paying to be here, but we're paying top dollar, and I believe part of the money is to go to some pet project you're running in the town so, whether you like it or not, you're expected to cooperate. Today, I need to get to know the layout of the place and organise the crew. From tomorrow, you're stuck with me. A shadow, however unwelcome.'

Jena watched the silvery grey eyes narrow and guessed he was contemplating another yell. Inwardly, she was regretting the foolish whim that had urged her to allow him to change the car tyre. He'd already been angry, and she'd made him angrier. Not the best of possible starts for someone who had hoped to win him over—or, at least, gain his cooperation.

Though how was she to know the doctor who'd been so against the filming would live at the end of nowhere?

Or be so good-looking?

Mentally scolding herself for the momentary distraction, she launched into her prepared speech.

'As the contract explained, this office isn't suitable so we'll be building a similar set-up—purely for the shots of you doing paperwork—in the space upstairs. Also a mock-up of the operating theatre, again for long shots.'

'And this is "real-life" television?'

She ignored his sniping comment, remembering instead the

question that had puzzled her since the location scouts had come up with a list of five possible hospitals within a day's drive of the city. All with space to build, if necessary, some extra sets.

'Why have hospitals shrunk so much you have an entire floor unoccupied? Are fewer people getting sick?'

If he was startled by the conversational switch he didn't show it, merely studying her for an instant before replying, 'Regional hospitals have altered their focus from primary care to providing a wider spread of services to more of the population, but they offer less specialised services.'

He paused, his fingers reaching for a pen which he then flipped from hand to hand as he continued, 'Which means that, as well as the trauma emergencies, cancer and major surgery patients also go to the city. Many of the surgery patients return here for post-surgical nursing, and we provide the facilities for follow-up testing for the cancer patients.'

Jena was mesmerised by his long fingers, carelessly playing with the pen. Better than being mesmerised by gleaming grey eyes, she decided, then reminded herself to listen to what he was saying. After all, she'd asked the question.

'To fully understand the changes in demographics, you have to realise that hospital stays are also much shorter these days,' he continued, his velvety voice making the words sound less like a lecture, the edge of anger she'd heard earlier fading as he talked about something he'd obviously considered himself.

'Fifty years ago, when hospitals like this were built, a patient lay in bed for three weeks after an appendix operation. Today a person is mobile within twenty-four hours and usually discharged from hospital within a couple of days. A hip injury which might have required three months in traction is now pinned or plated, perhaps both, and the patient can be weight-bearing within a few days, walking on a frame within a week.'

Despite a surprising fascination with lean fingers and a velvety voice, Jena absorbed what he was saying, but also recalled what she'd read in Noah Blacklock's biographical information, put together by someone in the research department.

'Then why would someone like yourself, with all your experience in emergency care, take a job in a country town where the medical needs of the patients are more of a nursing nature? Did you suffer burn-out in the city?'

He frowned, making her regret the question. And why should she care anyway? Her job was to establish a good working relationship with the man, and do a preliminary plan for the filming, not analyse him.

'I doubt that's your concern,' he said, and in case she'd missed the frown he underlined the words with a grimness she couldn't mistake. 'You were saying you'll only be using the top floor for your mock office and theatre, but your crew will need access to it, so unless they can levitate, they'll be passing through the foyer and up the stairs. Can I ask them to use the back entrance, and not make too much noise as they come and go?'

Jena had felt her muscles tighten at the sarcasm in his 'levitate' remark, but hoped her reaction hadn't shown. This was not a man to whom one could safely reveal any weakness.

The puzzle of why he'd come to Kareela remained, though that was, as he'd succinctly told her, none of her business.

'Our staff will all be briefed on moving quietly and not chattering on the stairs, minimising noise as much as possible,' she assured him. 'The set designer and carpenters will check out the top floor later today. I'll speak to them as soon as they arrive. It's possible that any heavy equipment and the bulk of the props they'll need can be hoisted up and lifted through windows rather than carried up the stairs.'

He didn't exactly look pleased—perhaps he didn't have a pleased look he could use—but he nodded, which was as close as she was likely to get to acceptance.

She was about to explain the other measures she'd put in place to ensure minimum disruption to the hospital when there was a brisk tap on the door, and it opened to admit a trim young man and an anorexic-looking but gym-toned blonde.

CHAPTER TWO

JENA caught the pained look on the doctor's face and wondered which of the newcomers had caused it. The blonde? Did all women upset him?

'I understood we were to sit in on the meeting with Miss Carpenter,' the man said stiffly. He propped himself against the desk and glared at Noah Blacklock.

Two angry men!

'And I understood the whole point of having a liaison was so that I only had to deal with one person during this circus—not a whole tribe of hangers-on.'

The woman sighed and shook her head.

'It's not your hospital, Noah,' she said, in a voice that suggested the words had been used a dozen times before.

Hadn't Jena herself used them earlier?

So why did she feel sorry for the doctor?

She glanced his way, saw thinned lips with a whiteness around them which suggested simple anger might have turned to rage.

'It really is much easier if I deal with one person,' Jena said, hoping to divert another explosion of wrath. 'Though, naturally, I'll be available for consultation with any of the staff. In fact, Dr Blacklock was about to take me around and introduce me to them.'

She stood up and held out her hand, first to the woman.

'Jena Carpenter,' she said, introducing herself while the doctor extricated himself from the clutter of papers that had fallen off his desk earlier.

'I'm Linda Carthew,' the blonde said, ignoring the hand and glaring at Jena as if she'd brought the plague.

Great! Another local who hates my guts! And if the glares continue, I'll have to start wearing sunglasses indoors.

The weak joke calmed her slightly.

'I'm Jeff Finch,' the man said. He grabbed the hand Linda Carthew had rejected and pumped it far too enthusiastically. 'I'm the administrative officer at the hospital—in charge of the overall running of the place—so anything you want, just ask. Linda is the most active member of our hospital board and was instrumental in gaining the board's approval for the filming to take place here.'

So the glare wasn't connected to the film crew, Jena thought, eyeing the woman to see if maybe she'd been wrong about the apparent animosity. Then Noah Blacklock reached her side, a kind of growling noise emanating from low down in his throat. Jena forgot Linda Carthew to concentrate on the immediate danger.

'Ms Carpenter is *my* liaison person!' Noah said grimly, then he seized Jena's elbow and steered her out of his office, across the reception area and into the main hospital foyer.

'*My* liaison person?' Jena echoed, hoping her voice didn't reveal the sudden attack of breathlessness the rushed exit must have caused.

'You know what I mean!' He was growling again. 'You're here to see to the welfare of the patients in this circus, not pander to that shiny-tailed pen-pusher or the celebrity-chasers on the board.'

His tone of voice, as well as his choice of words, left her in no doubt about what he thought of the pair they'd left in his office. The breathlessness she'd felt earlier was nothing compared to the total panic now reverberating through her chest. What had seemed like a relatively easy job was turning into a nightmare—before it had even begun.

'You know,' she said, wiggling her arm to remind him he was still gripping her elbow, 'when I came up here, spending the three weeks in Matt's old shack loomed as the major challenge of the location. I had no idea I was going to be caught up in a civil war.'

She turned towards him as she spoke and Noah saw the apprehension in her eyes.

'It's hardly that!' he said gruffly, then remembered it was pretty close.

'Well, not as far as the film project is concerned,' he amended. 'I might have been against it in the beginning but, you're right, I needed money for something else and agreed because of the financial inducement.'

He studied her again but, as far as he could see, the denim eyes were no less wary.

The woman was genuinely worried.

'I won't cause you any problems,' he promised.

Her smile broke through like sun through clouds, and she shook her head, making the strands of flaxen hair which had escaped the knot glimmer in the dim light of the foyer.

'No?' The teasing smile accompanying the word pressed the slit of a dimple into her right cheek.

He reined back a brief diversionary thought about the possibility of other dimples on Ms Carpenter's delectable body, and put some distance between them once again.

'Not if you don't cause me any,' he said, grumbling the words so she realised his moment of weakness had passed. 'Now, come along, I haven't got all day. I'll introduce you to whoever's on duty and find someone to take you around so you can see the layout of the place.'

He stalked off through a door on the right of the foyer, and Jena, puzzled by his mood swings, followed.

'Rhoda Dent, Sister-in-Charge,' Noah said, stopping by the nurses' station and waving his hand towards the woman sitting at the computer.

'I'm Jena Carpenter,' Jena offered when she realised the doctor had no intention of making a proper introduction.

She glanced towards him, and guessed it wasn't rudeness this time. His attention had been diverted by something on a piece of paper he'd picked up off the desk.

'Tom Jackson admitted Carla Trantino last night?' he said, looking past Jena to the nursing sister.

'He didn't leave you a message?' Rhoda murmured, scanning her desk as if a message might have been overlooked.

'Could have done,' Noah muttered. 'I tipped over a lot of papers—might have missed something that had been on top.' His eyes were again studying the paper as if some hidden meaning might be gleaned form whatever was written there. 'What happened?'

'No drugs,' Rhoda said swiftly. 'Well, not as far as anyone could tell. Tom felt a blood test would have been invasive— would have sent the wrong message to Carla.'

'That we didn't trust her?' Noah nodded, while Jena tried to guess what was happening. Tom Jackson was obviously another of the town's doctors but, from Rhoda's reassuring response about drugs, could Carla be a drug addict?

In a country town?

'Good for Tom!' Noah continued, leaving Jena no wiser. 'I knew he'd backed me in the project but hadn't realised he was wholeheartedly behind it.'

'His favourite cousin died of an overdose,' Rhoda said quietly. 'But Carla's problem was more a physical thing. Apparently a couple of local idiots decided the girls at your place were fair game and walked in expecting a party. The intruders had had too much to drink and had brought more alcohol with them. According to Tom, who had it from the lad called Davo, one of them grabbed Suzy by the arm and when Suzy screamed, all Carla's street-survival skills came into action.'

'It's a wonder it's not the local lads in hospital,' Noah said, but he shook his head as if the offhand remark did nothing to ease whatever pain this conversation was causing.

He cut across the room to a bed at the far end, and Jena, sensing her presence would be even less welcome than the film crew's, waited by the desk. Perhaps Rhoda would explain what was going on—or would she? Wasn't there such a thing as patient confidentiality?

'This is the women's ward and behind us are the men,' Rhoda said, not explaining but motioning with her head to another long, airy room, visible through a wide arch. 'Both have doors off the main hall, but because the stairs go up this side of the men's ward door, you don't notice it.'

Jena pictured the entry and wide hall in her mind.

'On the other side, behind the reception and office area,

there's an operating theatre and Casualty, which has its own entrance out the back.'

A younger nurse came in at that moment, and Rhoda signalled to her to join them.

'Jill, this is Jena Carpenter from the film company. Will you take her on a guided tour of the place and introduce her to all the staff while I walk round with Noah?'

Jill, a plump pretty young woman with reddish hair and the freckled skin it usually accompanied, looked delighted.

'We've all been dying for the filming to start. I know Noah says the whole idea is to act as normally as possible but, honestly, in a place this size, the Christmas street parade's exciting—so you can imagine what it's like having a television crew putting our hospital on *Real Life*!'

Her bubbly enthusiasm restored some of Jena's equilibrium. Or perhaps getting out of sight of Noah Blacklock had done it?

Jill led her across the ward and out through wide French doors onto an enclosed verandah.

'We call these the verandah beds for obvious reasons,' Jill said, smiling and waving her fingers at an elderly woman who was sitting up in the first bed. 'Hi, Mrs Nevins.'

The woman smiled but didn't reply, her attention focussed on the pattern of the brightly coloured wool she was knitting into an intricate pattern.

Drawn by the colours, Jena would have liked to have stopped, but Jill swept her onward, mentioning the names of other elderly patients as they passed.

'It's a kind of a stabilising and non-urgent care area,' Jill explained. 'People in for tests and trials of treatment. We've three GPs in town, and most of the people on the verandah are their patients rather than public patients. We've five private rooms, but the locals seem to prefer being on the verandah with other people, rather than shut away in rooms on their own. We use three of the private rooms for maternity suites now, though we don't have many babies delivered here. The town has an excellent midwife, so many women are opting for home births.'

Jena tried to absorb this flood of information, while mentally drawing her own rough floor plan of the hospital. When Jill led her off the verandah through a different set of French doors, she expected to come into the men's ward but instead found herself in a brightly decorated space more in keeping with a child-care centre than a hospital.

'This is our outpatient department. When Noah came it had the same pale green paint and tan linoleum as the rest of the hospital, but he checked through the stats and decided more kids came here than adults, so why not make it kid-friendly?'

'It's certainly worked,' Jena remarked, looking around in wonder at the vivid transfers on the walls and the bright mobiles hanging from the ceiling.

'Mr Finch didn't want to spend money on what he thought was a foolish idea so there was a bit of an argument about it. In the end, Noah did the work himself—with a bit of help from the yardman and the nurses. Now the grown-ups like it, too,' Jill assured her. She waved her hand towards treatment tables set against the wall. 'We have physios and occupational therapists who visit fortnightly and a speech pathologist who comes once a month. They use the room as a treatment room, which explains why it sees more kids than adults.'

Jena nodded to show she'd understood, but the image of the Noah Blacklock slapping on paint and sticking bright decals on the wall was a bit hard to accept—and she was still puzzled over the layout of the place.

'But where's the men's ward?' she asked, and Jill chuckled.

'Back this way,' she said, leading Jena through an internal door which took them into the corridor and eventually into the wide hall behind the stairs. 'On this lower floor, the building bumps out into a T-shape, so you go off the verandah straight into Outpatients. We walked past the door into Men's. The private rooms are on the verandah section on the other side.'

She then walked Jena at a bewildering pace through the series of small rooms filling the crosspiece of the T—equipment rooms, pharmacy, linen store, a huge kitchen where the smell of sweet buns baking made Jena's mouth water, then to the other side where X-Ray, scrub rooms, a well-equipped theatre and recovery room were all nestled side by side. Across from them was another ward where post-surgical patients, either minor cases treated at the hospital or those recuperating from operations in the city, were nursed.

In the same section as that occupied by the colourful Outpatients, on the other side was Casualty, empty now but looking ready for any emergency.

'Ha! I've found you. Jill show you everything? Was there anything else you needed to know?'

Did her reaction to Noah Blacklock's presence count as an emergency?

And why was he suddenly so cheerful, even helpful, when he'd made it plain earlier he was against all she stood for?

'Jill's been very kind, and I've met the cook who must surely be the most important member of the staff,' she said, hoping this amiable version of the doctor might be persuaded to remain.

'It's fairly rare to find a fully operational hospital kitchen so close to the city,' he agreed—agreeably! 'Most places get catered food delivered on a contract basis. Fortunately, Kareela had a heritage of good hospital food and a legacy of reliable kitchen staff. Mrs Meldrum's been here for thirty years.'

Jill murmured something about getting back to work and slipped away, leaving Jena uncertain what to do next.

'I'm sure you've also got work to do,' she said to Noah, who glanced at his watch and shrugged.

'Not for twenty minutes when an outpatient session begins. Would you like a cup of coffee?'

While she might, at first, have been surprised by his change in demeanour, Jena now found herself suspicious of it.

Highly suspicious.

She peered at him but could read nothing in a face which might have been hewn from fine-grained granite, so little did it reveal.

'OK!'

He didn't react to the half-heartedness of her agreement, merely nodding his head in the direction of the kitchen then leading the way.

He must want something. That was the only possible explanation for such a change—unless, of course, he was a practising schizophrenic!

Noah led the way towards the kitchen, his mind working furiously as he debated how he could draw Miss Liaison Person into helping Carla plan the group's contribution to the Christmas street parade.

'So, taking it easy, are you?' Mrs Meldrum asked, as he led Jena into the kitchen. 'And about time. How are things out at the lake? Sure you don't want to reconsider and shift into my spare room?'

'Quite sure, Mrs M.,' he replied. 'The shack's comfortable enough for a short-term stay.'

He was surprised to find he actually meant it. Though he'd been furious when Linda's machinations had necessitated his move out of town, the few days he'd already had out by the lake had been surprisingly restful. Until last night when a phone call from his sister, demanding to know his Christmas plans and telling him exactly what his nieces and nephews required in the way of gifts, had disturbed his sleep. Then he'd overslept so this morning he'd been running late…

Setting the memory of *that* folly firmly aside, he picked up the conversation before the women could wonder if he'd fallen asleep.

'Anyway, there's far too much excitement in town for the likes of me.'

'I heard what those hooligans did,' the cook replied. 'Young Brett Ward was one of them. I'll have something to say to his mother, you see if I don't.'

She turned to Jena and added, 'Sorry. You haven't a clue what we're talking about, have you? Country town stuff, that's all it is.'

Jena looked from the motherly woman to the man whose mood had switched so swiftly and waited for more of an explanation, but the cook was offering a choice of the fresh buns, hot from the oven, or biscuits she'd baked yesterday.

'You have to have something with your tea or coffee,' she

told Jena, waving her to a chair at a large, well-scrubbed table. 'Bad to be drinking caffeine on an empty stomach.'

'Is that a medical fact?' Jena asked Noah, who grinned at her as he replied.

'I think caffeine habits are probably bad whether you eat with it or not, but that doesn't stop me downing plenty of Mrs Meldrum's brew. It's good,' he added, as if he felt it necessary to assure her of the quality.

She tried to concentrate on the words, but the smile had caused a shift in her internal dynamics so she was busy reappraising her initial perceptions of the man.

Which was better than considering her physical reactions to him.

Caffeine—that's what they were discussing.

'I'm sure your coffee's excellent, and I'd love one of those fresh buns,' Jena said, concentrating hard on the woman who ran the kitchen. 'The smell of them cooking has been tantalising me.'

Mrs Meldrum pushed two mugs, a coffeepot and a plate of buns, halved and buttered so the butter was melting into the fresh dough and glazing the currants, across the table towards where Jena sat.

She reached for the coffeepot and poured herself a cup, then stretched across the table for milk and sugar. Giving Noah Blacklock, who'd settled into the chair next to her, long enough to take up the conversation.

He failed to take advantage of the opportunity, but Jena wasn't going to help out again. She took a bun and bit into it, the pleasure of the simple tastes so strong she wanted to moan with sheer delight.

She tried the coffee—it lived up to Noah's praise—and finished the piece of bun.

'The set designer and carpenters will be here at eleven,' she said when it became apparent Noah had forgotten why he'd invited her for coffee. 'I'll speak to them about moving quietly.'

He frowned at her, as if trying to remember who she was, then asked, 'What exactly will you be doing?' He hesitated, then added, 'I mean, I know you're to liaise between the television crew and me, but when there's no liaising to be done—like now—what's your job?'

'This week, I'll be following you and other staff around, getting a feel for the routines. When it goes to air, the programme will appear to have been shot in a week, but the actual filming is scheduled to take a fortnight then bits will be cut—'

'Real-life TV?' he murmured again, but less aggressively this time.

She grinned at him.

'I doubt there's any such thing, but it will be more real than *Country Hospital*, the show they'll use for comparisons!'

Then, because grinning at him didn't seem like such a good idea, she turned her attention back to his question.

'Once I've got some idea of what your usual day entails, and have a feel for the hospital routine, I'll do a suggested filming schedule.'

'Doctor arrives at work, doctor saves life, doctor delivers baby—'

'Doctor gets a sock on the jaw!' Jena warned. 'And the show isn't about you, it's about the hospital, the staff and the patients.'

'You can do that—work out filming schedules?' he asked, sounding genuinely puzzled.

Jena hoped her reaction hadn't shown on her face. After all, Noah Blacklock wasn't the first person to doubt she had a brain.

Though this time it irritated her far more than usual...

Not wanting to go there, she took a deep breath and explained.

'I've been involved in television production for eighteen months so I have some idea of what works and what doesn't,' she said. 'I began as a general dogsbody, helping out wherever I was needed, then moved on to production assistant. This will be much the same, only my primary concern will be keeping an eye on the crew once filming starts so the hospital staff and patients aren't inconvenienced.'

'Which shouldn't be too difficult once you've explained what you want them to do?'

The question hung in the air between them, loaded with undercurrents Jena couldn't understand.

Unless...

Memories of losing the job she'd really wanted flashed through her head—the producer's voice saying, 'I know you're more than a pretty face, Jena, but other people's perception of you will be different. The general public would see you as a beautiful blonde but not credit you with brains, and the show would lose veracity.'

Sitting in the hospital kitchen, anger now fizzed where attraction had briefly flickered.

'You're saying even a blonde should be able to manage it?' she fumed, standing up and pushing back her chair with her calves. 'Talk about stereotypical thinking!'

'No, not at all!'

Noah was also on his feet, and almost stuttering in his haste to deny her assumption.

'It was nothing like that. Just the free time. I was thinking you might have free time.'

'Not to spend with you! Not if my life depended on it!' Jena snorted, then she stormed out of the room, down the hall and up the stairs, only realising when she reached the top that she'd have to go back down again to meet the crew.

Having them blundering around the place, talking loudly, was hardly the way to convince Noah Blacklock she'd be doing a first-class job!

Also, she hadn't properly investigated the back of the building to see how feasible it would be for the cast and crew to enter and leave that way.

She peered over the railing to see if the coast was clear. A nurse swept across her field of vision, but there was no sign of the aggravating doctor.

Creeping down the stairs like a timid rabbit was out of the question, but she needn't make a lot of noise. Not if she took her time.

'Oh, there you are. I'd like to talk to you.'

Linda Carthew spoke as if she'd been searching the premises for Jena for some hours. Where she'd come from, Jena couldn't guess—though it was a day for sudden appearances and disappearances so she shouldn't have been surprised by Linda materialising at the foot of the steps.

'Yes, Ms Carthew?'

Jena hoped she sounded polite, although the woman's terse demand had raised her hackles—again!

'Call me Linda. It's about this liaison business. You're supposed to be the liaison between the hospital and the film crew, and the hospital includes the board and the administrator.'

Jena thought back to what the producer had told her about this job and knew trouble lay ahead.

'Actually,' she replied as she reached the hall and could stand face to face with the woman, 'I was appointed as liaison between the medical staff, under Dr Blacklock, and the television company, although, of course, we could include a board meeting and the discussions which take place there as well.'

She tried to make the words sound inconsequential, hoping to avoid a confrontation, but she guessed Linda wouldn't be easily appeased.

'Dr Blacklock is the board's employee!' Linda snorted, proving Jena's guess correct.

'Really?' Jena murmured, determined to remain calm while she launched herself straight at the woman's jugular. 'I understood he was employed by the State Health Department, which is why the original negotiations for the use of Kareela Hospital were conducted through them and the Minister. Of course, out of consideration for the local people, the board and key staff at the hospital were also consulted.'

Linda opened her mouth, then closed it again. Apparently, the power of the government still held some sway, and the mention of ministerial support had silenced her.

At that moment, Jena caught sight of a gaggle of men and women heading towards the front door.

'Excuse me,' she said to Linda, and she slipped away, across the hall and out the door, hurrying down the front steps to intercept the scruffy-looking group before they could come in.

Ritual hugs and loud cries of 'Darling!' greeted her, and by the time she'd detached herself from the last hugger they were at the bottom of the front steps.

Noah Blacklock was at the top—Linda Carthew nowhere in sight.

CHAPTER THREE

NOAH could think of no reason why he found the attire of the film crew so offensive—after all, why shouldn't they wear flowered board shorts and scruffy, paint-stained T-shirts? But Noah thought the scene so distasteful he scowled at the woman who glanced towards him.

She scowled right back and shook her head as if to say, Buzz off! I'm handling it!

He ignored the silent message and stood his ground, folding his arms and scowling harder.

'OK, gang,' he heard her say, spreading her arms to prevent them mounting the steps. 'Mr Happy up there is the medical superintendent of this hospital and he doesn't want us trooping in and out through the main entrance, making a noise and disturbing his patients.'

'Mr Happy?' one of the crew echoed doubtfully. Another punched Jena lightly on the shoulder and said, 'Way to go, girl! I knew you'd make the perfect liaison person—such tact and diplomacy.'

'I can be diplomatic when I want but it doesn't always work,' Noah heard Jena retort. 'Like now! Will you lot get your sorry selves around the back of this building forthwith?'

She herded them along the path which, if she had but known it, would merely lead them to Outpatients. Eventually, she might find the back entrance to the building—once they'd negotiated the incinerator, various outhouses and the brick shed housing the emergency generator.

Time to take control?

'If you've got equipment, you'd be better off going back to your vehicles, driving out of the car park, turning left down the first side road and in through another gate. You'll find a staff car park with plenty of space, and the back door leads off it.'

34

Jena turned to stare at him.

Surprised by his helpfulness, or annoyed by his interference?

'Thanks!' she said, and briefly flashed a smile that made the day seem brighter.

Which was an observation fraught with danger.

She let the crew wander back towards their cars and came up the steps.

'I apologise for the "Mr Happy" remark,' she said, then, just as he was about to offer his own apology for scowling, she spoilt it by adding, 'but you *were* standing there looking like a thundercloud, and the crew hadn't even reached the steps.'

'The back door's down the hall, then left into the narrower corridor then right. You should be able to find it easily enough.'

'Even though I'm blonde?' she sniped at him, and he found himself growling again.

Though beneath the anger he wondered about her edginess—about the 'blonde' references. Had someone, in this day and age of enlightenment and political correctness, used her looks against her? Or did the old 'dumb blonde' attitude hold more sway than he'd realised in the public's mind?

Jena hurried through the hall, sorry she'd given in to the impulse to have the last word. And the 'Mr Happy' impulse earlier. Why was she behaving so irrationally towards the man when she was supposed to be a soothing influence, not an exacerbating one?

Because grey eyes with the sheen of polished steel caused tremors down her spine? Seemed to penetrate her skin and leave her flesh uneasy?

Or because he was as changeable as the wind—one minute being helpful and suggesting coffee, the next treating her as if her presence in his life was anathema to him.

She put the puzzle of Noah Blacklock from her mind, found the back door and once again intercepted the crew—three men and a woman, three of them familiar from previous shoots.

'OK—here are the rules,' she told them, when they'd teased

her about kowtowing to the doctor. 'Minimum noise inside the building—on the stairs and in the corridors and hall. As much of the carpentry work as possible should be done outside.'

She looked around at the rear parking area.

'There's plenty of space out here.'

'We've got the mobile workshop coming up later today and also a hoist, so heavy gear like the dollies and cameras we'll use upstairs can be hoisted straight up and swung through a window,' Andrew Watts, the props officer on the project, told her. 'I sussed it all out when I came up earlier.'

'It's only when people are tramping up and down the steps there's likely to be any noise,' Kate Jennings, the site manager, remarked.

They were standing at the bottom of the steps, looking up, all of them considering the number of people who were involved in even the shortest of scenes.

'Most people wear trainers, so the actual footsteps won't be noisy, but you can't stop people talking to each other.'

'Anyone sick enough to be bothered by a little human conversation is sent to the city hospital,' a quavery voice said, and Jena turned to find one of the verandah patients standing behind them. It was the knitter, Mrs Nevins, knitting needles still in hand, wool in her dressing-gown pocket and the bright bundle of completed fabric tucked under one arm.

'The rest of us are looking forward to a bit of liveliness around the place. Very depressing, hospitals can be. I know the staff all do their best, but it's not much fun, you know, being surrounded by sick people.'

Jena was so relieved to hear this opinion that she smiled at the woman.

'Thank you,' she said, and meant it, though she knew the warning for the cast and crew to behave with consideration and decorum would still have to be repeatedly enforced.

'The town's behind you, too,' Mrs Nevins continued. 'Not like they were about Noah's druggies, although I can't see any harm in the poor young things living here if it might help them stay off the drugs.'

Noah's druggies?

The words puzzled Jena and she wanted to question them, but she felt it might not be prudent to gossip about the person with whom she was liaising on her very first day on the job.

'I'll see you later, Mrs Nevins,' Jena told her. 'Right now, I'd better take the crew upstairs.'

Mrs Nevins nodded, but made no move to return to her bed on the verandah. She waited until the motley group had spread out up the staircase before adding, 'There's a ghost up there. They say the hospital closed the floor because of numbers but it was the ghost. Old Dr Granger's wife, it is.'

She tucked her knitting more firmly under her arm and turned away, her slippers making no sound on the tiled floor. Only the click of her knitting needles, growing fainter, indicated her departure.

Great! Jena thought as she followed the chuckling members of the crew up the stairs. Now we've got a ghost as well as an unwelcoming doctor.

She was smiling to herself over the silly thought when a loud cry diverted her thoughts from ghosts and the doctor. She took the remaining steps two at a time, intending to yell, quietly, at whoever had made the noise. She was willing to bet there'd be ghost sightings among the crew on a daily basis, now the ghost's presence was known.

But it wasn't a ghost which had caused the loud cry. That much was obvious when Jena reached the top landing and took one look at the white-faced woman who sat there, clutching her left shoulder and moaning pitifully.

'What on earth happened?' Jena demanded, turning to the rest of the group for an explanation.

'Something hit me on the shoulder. It's broken for sure.' Kate was the one who answered, so apparently no one else had seen the accident.

Jena looked around and saw what had probably caused the problem, though the crew's wary attitudes suggested they were ready to lay the blame on the ghost.

'There's a wrought-iron bracket on the wall. It probably held trays at one time.' She pointed out this obstruction to

Kate as she knelt beside the young woman. 'You must have been turning to talk to someone and walked into it.'

As she spoke, Jena studied the affected shoulder. Though it was years since she'd done the prac. work in her nursing training, she could see a loss of contour in Kate's shoulder which suggested a dislocation. She hadn't seen the bracket so hadn't been facing that way, but if she'd struck it front on, a dislocation was likely.

'Well, at least you chose a good place to have an accident,' Jena told her. 'Do you want me to get someone to bring a stretcher or can you walk back down the stairs?'

'I'll walk,' Kate said grimly. The haste with which she rose to her feet, and the apprehension in her eyes as she looked around, suggested she hadn't accepted Jena's logical explanation of the accident.

Jena turned to Andrew. 'Could you and Brad help Kate down the stairs? Don't touch her arm or shoulder. I'll get the doctor.'

She slipped away from them, mentally rehearsing what she would say to Noah Blacklock. How to present him with a new patient within an hour of the advance crew's arrival, after assuring him he'd barely notice the crew in 'his' hospital.

She found him in the men's ward, sitting on a chair pulled up beside the bed of a young boy.

Playing chess.

'I'm sorry to disturb you, Dr Blacklock,' she said, using his formal title in these surroundings. 'But one of the crew's had an accident…'

Her voice tailed away but fortunately the boy took over, lifting the chessboard carefully from the side of the bed and placing it on his locker.

'Serves you right, Noah! Off you go. I'll work out a way to get out of check while you're gone.'

He grinned at the doctor, who was grumbling about losing this one chance to beat him, but although the smile made the small face come alive, it did nothing to disguise the signs of chronic illness on the child's face.

'What's wrong with him?' she asked, as Noah accompanied her out of the ward.

'Shouldn't you be more concerned with your own patient?' Noah snapped. 'I assume it's something serious or you wouldn't have disturbed me.'

His reaction sparked one in Jena.

'Not when you were obviously snowed under with work,' she snapped right back at him.

They'd reached the hall, and met the cluster of crew members surrounding the injured Kate.

'I think it's a dislocated shoulder, anterior dislocation,' Jena continued in her coolest tones. Then for pure devilment she added, 'The ghost did it.'

The look of horror on Noah's face told Kate she'd struck a nerve, but his concern when he looked at Kate's shoulder, the gentleness of his hands as he felt the joint, made her feel mean for doing it.

She shooed the rest of the crew back upstairs, reminding them they had jobs to do and not much time in which to do them.

'I'll be up later,' she promised, then walked behind Kate and Noah towards the casualty room.

'We'll X-ray it first,' Noah explained to Kate, 'just to check there are no broken bones, then I'll give you a light anaesthetic and pop it back into place.'

Jena gave an inward shudder. 'Popping it back into place' sounded easy, but she remembered enough of her training to know it could only be reduced either by moving the arm, flexed at the elbow, in horribly awkward contortions or by the surgeon putting his foot, minus the shoe, into the shoulder joint and somehow levering the head of the humerus out until the muscles surrounding it pulled it back into its correct position.

'Read about the Hippocratic method of reduction, did you?' Noah asked; and Jena realised her shudder must have been outward as well as inward.

'Do you use that method?' she asked him, as she accompanied the pair into the X-ray room.

'No! I find it a bit violent. The four-step Kocher method does me.'

'Hey, you guys, it's my shoulder we're talking about here. What's going on?'

Kate was pale with pain but had recovered enough equilibrium to join the conversation.

'We're discussing different ways of getting it back into place,' Jena told her, then she shot a teasing look at Noah before giving more reassurance. 'Dr Blacklock *seems* to know what he's doing.'

'What does it mean?' Kate asked. 'As far as work goes? I don't want to lose this job.'

She sounded panicky and Jena was pleased when Noah reassured her.

'Three weeks in a complicated kind of sling, that should do it. It's mainly to give the torn tendons time to heal. You'll be able to use your fingers and hand but the sling will keep the shoulder stable.'

'And tonight? I can go home, well, back to the motel, tonight?'

'Let's take the X-ray and see how bad it is,' Noah said gently. 'I'd actually prefer to have you stay overnight in the hospital if it won't be inconvenient for you, in case of complications.'

'What complications?' Kate demanded, and Jena glanced at Noah, wondering just how honestly he'd answer.

'There could be injury to the nerves around the joint which would result in a loss of feeling in your arm. There could be injury to a vein or an artery, causing internal bleeding we'd pick up if you were in hospital. Also, the X-ray could show an injury to one of the small bones in the shoulder, but if we stop chatting and take the pictures I might be able to rule it out right now.'

A nurse Jena hadn't met appeared from the direction of Casualty.

'Heard voices and thought you might need me,' she said. 'Dislocated shoulder? You want lateral as well as anteroposterior shots?'

'Definitely,' Noah told her, then let her lead Kate into the small room and position her, seated, on the table.

'Did you meet Marion?' he asked Jena. 'Positive genius with an X-ray machine. Well, with this particular machine, which, as far as I'm concerned, should have been consigned to the trash about ten years ago. However, Marion can coax spectacular results from the antiquated old thing and as the Health Department is starting to believe even cases needing an X-ray should be transported elsewhere, I won't be getting a new one in the foreseeable future.'

Jena heard impatience in his voice and wondered if this centralisation of services aggravated him. Yet he'd apparently chosen to come to work in Kareela, knowing it already existed. He must have applied for the position, as people of his rank in medical circles didn't get transferred willy-nilly.

Unless…

The phrase she'd heard earlier, 'Noah's druggies', echoed in her mind, but a sneaky glance at his strong profile confirmed her earlier impression. The man looked far too alert and fit and healthy to have had anything to do with drugs.

As another premonitory shiver slithered down her spine, Jena turned her attention to Marion, who was positioning Kate ready for the X-ray.

'Out of here, you hangers-on,' Marion said, waving Jena and Noah from the room. 'I'll bring the negatives and your patient through to Theatre, Noah.'

Jena backed out of the small room and was about to walk away, knowing she should see the rest of the crew to let them know what was happening.

'I understood most of the television crew would be staying locally. Is there a problem for this lass if she stays in overnight?'

Noah's question reminded Jena of Kate's apparent concern over hospitalisation, but she couldn't work out what had caused it.

'I don't know,' she had to admit. 'Filming doesn't start until next week so the rest of the crew won't come until the weekend, but this lot are all booked into accommodation in the town.'

'Can you find out what the complication is?' Noah persisted, and Jena, realising liaising was a two-way street, nodded.

'I'll get back to you as soon as I can,' she promised.

Upstairs, she found the others working in almost total silence—a state so unusual in a film crew it worried Jena.

'Hey, guys,' she said. 'It's a dislocated shoulder, not the end of the world. Kate will be out of pain in half an hour and as good as new in three weeks.'

'I thought we were *supposed* to work quietly,' Andrew said, looking up from where he held a tape against a wall. He jotted another measurement in his notebook and waved his hand towards the others, all busy with their jobs.

And silent.

'It's not good, having an accident before shooting even begins,' he continued, and Jena closed her eyes and prayed for patience. Of all people on earth, theatre—and by extension film and television—people had to be the most superstitious.

'Kate walked into the bracket and hurt her shoulder,' she said, quite loudly, hoping to dispel the atmosphere straining the air in the room. 'No ghosts, no symbol of bad luck, just an accident, pure and simple. Now, are there any obvious problems that need the involvement of the hospital authorities? Andrew, have you checked on how the hoist will work, where you'll site it? I'll have to let them know about any external structures we're planning to erect.'

'John's in charge of the hoist,' Andrew replied. 'John, take Jena downstairs and show her what we've planned.'

John was the crew member she hadn't worked with before, so she was glad of an opportunity to spend some time with him. He looked absurdly young, but she'd realised when she'd first moved from modelling to the television world that most of the offsiders on any shoot were only in their late teens— early twenties at the most. Even Kate, with her important title of site manager, was barely twenty.

'What does it mean, this dislocated shoulder?' John asked,

and Jena, thinking the question was merely a polite enquiry about an injured colleague, proceeded to explain.

'No!' he said impatiently. 'What does it mean for her? Will they keep her in hospital and, if so, for how long? You said something about three weeks—will she be in pain all that time? Will it be hurting her?'

He sounded genuinely concerned, so Jena tried to reassure him, explaining the pain was worst when it happened, and although it might be uncomfortable for a while, mild analgesics would counter it.

The mention of possible hospitalisation reminded her of Noah's question about Kate's apparent concern. Maybe John could help.

'Do you know her well?'

They'd reached the bottom of the stairs and were walking through the hall, but even in the less than perfect light Jena saw the tide of colour wash into the young man's cheeks.

'Pretty well,' he said gruffly, lengthening his strides so Jena had to trot to keep up with him.

It took her another thirty minutes, in between technical discussions of where the hoist would be located and how it would be stabilised by inserting pins into the brickwork, to realise why Kate had been upset.

'They've been going out together, she and a young carpenter called John,' Jena explained, much later, to Noah. 'And, for young people these days, have been very…I guess restrained would be the word—'

'Young people? Are you so old that's how they seem to you?'

They were standing outside the recovery room, and the question made Jena smile.

'I'm twenty-seven,' she said bluntly. 'Not that much older in years maybe, but I feel about a hundred years older in experience.'

She felt her own cheeks heat as she realised how the phrase could have been taken, then plunged on into the explanation in the hope Noah wouldn't notice her pinkness.

'Anyway, it seems they'd had long and earnest discussions

about taking their relationship further—to a more intimate level.' She realised the heat certainly wasn't going to go away while she discussed this subject. She'd just have to ignore it. 'When they were both selected to go on location up here, they took it as a sign that things were meant to be.'

Jena hesitated. She didn't want Noah Blacklock mocking the earnest young couple, but if he was to understand why Kate was so worried…

'They decided to make it a kind of trial honeymoon,' she went on, and looked him straight in the eye, daring him to make a joke of it. 'Though he's more concerned about Kate and the pain she's in than missing out on a bit of sex.'

'He told you all this?' Noah asked, disbelief warring with a desire to laugh—although the challenge in Jena's eyes warned him that laughing would be a big mistake.

'Eventually,' she said, while the tender smile lurking in her eyes told him she'd also found the story more touching than amusing.

Twenty-seven but not as cynical as her remark about being 'a hundred years older in experience' had suggested she was.

A woman as beautiful as she had undoubtedly had her pick of lovers. The idea bothered him though he knew it shouldn't. Jena Carpenter's past—or future beyond these few weeks of filming—was no concern of his.

'Are we keeping Kate in hospital?'

Rhoda, who'd left the ward to assist with the operation and had been watching Kate in Recovery, emerged to ask the question.

'Just overnight,' Noah replied, 'but I'll tell her.' He turned to Jena. 'You'll come with me?'

'Sure,' she said, moving immediately towards the door, her blonde head higher than his shoulder as they walked side by side—a tall woman as well as a beautiful one.

'Just one night, Kate? To humour me?' Noah said to his patient, who was sitting up on the edge of the bed and glowering in response to his suggestion.

'Better than whoever's rooming with you at the motel having to race you up to the hospital in the middle of the night if something does go wrong,' Jena said, and Noah silently congratulated her on both her tact and her approach. One look at Kate's face was enough to tell him she didn't like the scenario at all.

He felt a pang of sympathy for the young would-be lovers. There was always so much uncertainty in the early stages of a relationship, and it was worse when one was young.

Wasn't it?

Not always, he reminded himself, thinking of his own blundering folly in seeing too much of Linda Carthew when he'd first arrived in Kareela, not realising she'd wanted more than friendship—and had expected more than that from him.

He couldn't use youth as an excuse for that mistake!

Or the consequences that were now making his life difficult!

He shook his head.

'You're sure it will only be one night?' Kate demanded, no doubt confused by his head shake.

'Unless something major goes wrong, which is most unlikely,' Noah promised her. 'Now, stay there and I'll get a wardsman. I know you could walk through to the ward, but hospital regulations say you should be wheeled. Rhoda will look after you when you get there.'

'I'll get the wardsman,' Rhoda offered, and she whisked out of the room.

'Do you want me to get anything from the motel? Toilet things? Nightdress?'

Jena asked the questions, speaking gently to the injured young woman, but Kate was recovering quickly.

'No, John will do it for me. John Jansen, he's with the crew,' she said, looking directly at Jena to tell her more than the words had said. 'Is it OK if he comes down to see me now?'

'Of course it is,' Jena told her, then she touched Kate lightly on her good arm. 'I'll let him know you'll be in the ward.'

'On the verandah,' Rhoda said, rejoining them, a young man in tan shirt and shorts accompanying her. 'I'll put you next to Mrs Nevins. She'll keep you amused, and probably occupied as well, sorting through her coloured wools.'

Noah watched as Jena left the room, then, feeling he wasn't needed by either Kate or Rhoda, he followed her out.

She was already halfway up the stairs and as he couldn't think of any good reason to go after her he let her go, idly noticing the flash of bare legs he could see through the banisters as she took the last flight two at a time.

No women and definitely no blondes, he reminded himself, then he turned to find the blonde who'd troubled him most recently hovering behind him.

'I understood you weren't interested in a relationship,' Linda said, sarcasm biting so sharply through the words Noah felt himself flinch. 'In fact, if I recall your words correctly—'

'Were you looking for me?' he interrupted, knowing the last thing he needed repeated in the hospital foyer was his stumbling explanation of why he didn't want to get involved with her.

'Yes!' she said, scowling at him to show she understood why he'd changed the subject but going along with it anyway. 'I heard there was trouble at your house last night.' She didn't bother to hide her satisfaction. 'One of those girls injured in a fight.'

Noah heard the personal spite in Linda's words and hesitated before answering. Her position on the hospital board didn't entitle her to patient information but did her 'day job' as a local councillor mean she'd see the police report?

He doubted it, and once again regretted the fact the police had been called, although he couldn't blame Suzy for alerting them. She'd have been terrified.

'Well?' Linda demanded.

'I don't see what it has to do with you,' Noah said slowly, although he knew he was stirring up trouble by refusing to answer. 'You made the point that you didn't want the halfway house in the town, but now it's here, why continue to make things difficult?'

He didn't say outright that he suspected it was personal. He guessed she was behind delaying his original plan to house the project in his aunt's old place. It seemed unlikely a council inspector had called at the house by accident—or found so many minor things wrong with it. Which had resulted in the young people living temporarily in his house while he stayed out at the lake.

'Surely you must believe these kids deserve a chance?'

Linda snorted, and stormed away, no doubt to add fuel to the flames already burning in Jeff Finch's heart, also caused by Noah Blacklock's presence in the town. Though Linda's animosity had only developed since Noah had backed away from a relationship with her, while Jeff's was motivated by ambition, and had been firmly in place before Noah arrived.

He walked back through to where Carla was recovering from the torn ligaments and concussion she'd suffered in the 'trouble'.

The young woman, as thin as a wraith beneath the sheet, was sleeping, tiny shudders in her body and a constant flickering of her eyelids suggesting the sleep was far from restful.

'She's dead scared the fight will spoil the chances of the town accepting the halfway house,' Jill said, coming to stand beside Noah as he looked down at the sleeping girl.

'And will it?' Noah asked.

The young nurse looked thoughtful, then at last she replied, 'I think people will be more behind it now, not less. Even those who didn't want it here wouldn't like to think it was local lads causing trouble. I mean, at first, when the backpackers started coming, everyone in town was up in arms, now they accept them like they're family.'

Noah smiled.

'Possibly something to do with the money they spend here,' he reminded Jill.

'I guess you're right, but it's brought the town alive again as well. I mean, there are dances now and bands come. Once you had to go to the city for any kind of night life.'

Noah nodded. He knew the contribution the backpackers had made to the town's resurgence. And now there were the television people…

Before he could ask Jill what she thought of the television crew being there, a young man arrived.

'John?'

The lad blushed and nodded, while Noah wondered if he'd ever been young enough to blush.

If so, it had been a long time ago.

'Kate's on the verandah,' he said, speaking gently. 'I think you'll be able to pick her out among our other patients.'

'I'll show you,' Jill volunteered, and Noah guessed the answer to the question he hadn't asked. Jill, like most of the town's people, would be delighted to have the television crew here. In this case, it was he who was the odd one out.

CHAPTER FOUR

'WHY didn't you want us here?'

Trust Jena Carpenter to put him on the spot. They were driving out towards the lake—or rather Noah was driving and Jena was his passenger, her ancient LandCruiser having refused to start and been left to the tender mercies of the local garage.

Noah could feel so many reasons piling up in his head that he sighed.

Jena heard the soft exhalation.

'Is it *so* difficult to answer?'

She was sitting as close to the door as she possibly could, frustration at her vehicle's untrustworthiness having given away to apprehension about having to travel to her temporary home, and consequently back to town tomorrow morning, with Noah Blacklock.

Not that she thought he'd bite—she just didn't want to be spending more time than necessary in his company. Neither did she want to have to analyse *that* particular resolve. She'd never experienced a physical attraction as instant as the one she'd felt for him. Ridiculous, when she considered she didn't like him as a person—or not from what she'd seen of him so far. While he certainly had no liking for her.

'Choose one reason and think about the rest,' she suggested, determined not to let him guess how uncomfortable she was feeling.

He shrugged, drawing her attention to his broad shoulders.

'Drugs,' he said, after a silence so long she'd decided he wasn't going to answer.

'Oh, great!' she muttered at him. 'The wonderful power of assumption. Think film or television crew and immediately the word "drugs" pops into your head.'

'Into other people's heads as well,' he protested. 'You must

49

admit, there seems to be an almost accepted level of drug culture among film and television people.'

'So, going on popular perception of this drug culture, you naturally assumed the entire crew would be stoned to the gills and, no doubt, pressing drugs on the innocent youth of Kareela.'

'Not at all,' he said, turning off the highway and swinging towards the little settlement. 'But I wondered if having a television crew in town, whether they were users or not, might not attract an undesirable element.'

'By which you mean pushers?' Jena said. She thought about this for a moment, then admitted, 'It's a logical concern, but is it yours? Surely it's the parents of the town's teenagers who should be voicing it.'

Her stomach scrunched as she realised she could well have put her foot in it. She shot a quick look at his left hand. She was sure she'd have noticed if he'd been wearing a wedding ring.

But not all men did.

Wasn't he too young to have teenage children?

'I doubt they gave it a thought,' Noah admitted. 'Most of the concern about the television crew was whether they'd buy their food locally or bring it all from the city.'

Jena sensed he'd deliberately changed the subject, but she answered anyway.

'Crews I've worked with always buy locally,' she assured him. 'A lot of film and television people are fanatical about what they eat. The word "fresh" features strongly in most of their dietary requirements.'

He must have heard a trace of cynicism in her voice, for he asked, 'Not into star theatrics, Miss Carpenter?'

'Not unnecessary ones,' Jena told him. 'I modelled for years and, believe me, that life is far tougher than an actor's, so throwing a tantrum over a black spot on a banana doesn't go down too well with me.'

'Do the so-called stars still do that?' he asked, his voice vibrant with disbelief.

'Not many do,' Jena admitted. 'Most are sane, normal people, whose job just happens to shed a certain aura around them—and attract a lot of often unwanted publicity.'

'And the same can't be said for models?' he asked, the grey gaze flicking sideways for a brief glance her way.

'Only those at the very top—the super models. Beneath them are thousands more whose names are virtually unknown.' She looked out of the window, seeking a diversionary topic. One which might prove as successful as his had, she realised. He'd turned her completely away from her enquiry about his reaction to the television crew's arrival in the town.

They were driving more slowly now, along the rutted sandy track. 'Do all these shrubs have flowers in spring? It must be beautiful during the wildflower season.'

He glanced her way again and grinned at her.

'Don't want to talk about modelling?'

'There's not much to say,' she said bluntly, then, guessing he would continue to pursue the subject, decided she'd get it over and done with.

'It's darned hard work, and generally uncomfortable, because you always have to be ahead of the seasons. For instance, swimsuit ads are made in the depths of winter and you can guarantee any time there's a beach shoot it will either be blowing a gale or raining.'

Noah was watching the road, his strong, capable hands easing the big four-wheel drive effortlessly through the sand. The look of polite enquiry on his face suggested he was waiting for more information, and as she found the silence unnerving Jena continued the short version of her autobiography.

'I took it up when I was at school, for pocket money, and kept myself when I was at university with part-time jobs. By the time I'd finished my degree and was ready to begin full-time at a hospital I was earning so much as a model, and had such good offers to work overseas, it seemed stupid not to keep doing it.'

'But you've stopped now.' Noah pointed out the obvious. Once again he glanced her way, his gaze sweeping over her. 'Get too old?'

She chuckled.

'If you want to offend me, you'll have to do better than that. Believe me, most models have been offended by experts. And, no, I didn't get so old I couldn't get plenty of work—I simply got tired of it. Tired of the travel, the working conditions, people's attitudes...'

She regretted the last admission the moment she'd made it, but losing the job she'd really wanted when she'd made the shift to television, for no other reason than the producer's perception of her as a 'face' rather than an intelligent being, still rankled. Inevitably, Noah echoed the words with a question mark at the end.

'Dumb-blonde syndrome!' she muttered at him. 'And don't bother asking what that is. I saw it reflected in your eyes this morning when you snatched the jack out of my hands.'

He didn't defend himself, but argued the assumption.

'Surely such thinking doesn't still exist? I know people make a joke of it, but blonde women are everywhere, from reporting on television to running companies.'

'Of course they're everywhere,' Jena said. 'After all, we make up a large portion of the world's population, but in the film and television world where so many models—mostly blonde—have tried to make it and failed, there are some lingering attitudes that can make life very difficult.'

She was tempted to tell him about the job she'd lost, but knew the story would sound pathetic to someone who hadn't suffered a major career setback.

Not that he seemed to expect further conversation on the topic, simply turning off the main track down the overgrown excuse for a drive that led to Matt's old holiday shack.

'What are you doing for water?' Noah asked, eyeing the loose weatherboards and sagging verandah with distaste. 'That tank's rusted right through.'

'I brought plenty with me,' Jena told him, feeling a slightly irrational need to defend her temporary home.

'And power?'

'I've got a gas bottle, a gas ring with a barbecue plate and a gas lamp.'

She opened the car door and got out, the uneasiness she was

feeling in his presence far stronger than her doubts about her primitive accommodation.

'Well, remind Matt that the ban on generators running after nine at night still exists and if I hear his going later, I'll come over and personally disable it.'

She'd been about to shut the car door when he added this threat, but this new reference to Matt made her open it again and poke her head inside the car.

'Not only is there no generator, Matt Ryan isn't here either. And he won't be,' she said firmly, then she retreated and again was about to shut the door—possibly with a slight slam—when Noah's hand prevented her. He'd leant across the passenger seat and was studying her face.

'Then what the hell are you doing out here?' he demanded. 'This place is a wreck. You could fall through a floor board, have moths and possums and possibly even flying foxes flitting about all night. You can't possibly *want* to live there.'

Jena suppressed a shudder. Moths she could cope with, even possums, but she had grave doubts about the flying foxes!

However, that wasn't Noah Blacklock's business, and there was no way she was going to reveal her fears to him, of all men.

She gave him her best smile, the one she used when the photographer wanted 'radiant' and said earnestly, 'Oh, but I do!'

He might not believe her but it was the truth. For the next three weeks she *did* want to live in the shack, to prove to herself as much as to Matt that she could do it.

He lifted his shoulders in a disbelieving way then, as she tried to shut the door, he exerted more pressure on it.

'You've got a mobile?'

She nodded.

'And my card?'

Another nod—surely it was somewhere in her handbag.

'If you walk down to the beach in front of the house, my place is about a hundred yards along to the right. You can't see it from here, but there's a cleared track running from it down to the beach so you should be able to find it easily enough.'

It wasn't exactly an invitation, but Jena was grateful to know there was someone close at hand so she smiled as she thanked him, and this time he let her shut the door.

Noah watched her climb cautiously up the wobbly steps to what remained of the verandah. One false move in the dark and she'd go straight through some of those floorboards.

Stubborn bloody woman! Why on earth was she staying there? To prove something seemed the likely answer, but to herself or someone else?

Matt Ryan?

Noah backed up and turned the Jeep, wondering if the anger he was feeling was a hangover from the days when Matt— Matt the perfect, Noah had dubbed him—had haunted his holidays. Surely it couldn't be anything else.

He roared off up the drive, turned onto his own track and slowed as he approached the little shack which had been his family's holiday home. Unlike the Ryans, his parents had spent money on the place, keeping it in good repair and using it at regular intervals even after their offspring had grown up.

Noah had recently taken over its upkeep, putting in solar cells and storage batteries so he rarely had to use the generator. But how could he sleep soundly in his comfortable bed when Jena was virtually camping out just a hundred yards away?

He went inside, checked his fridge and in the end pulled a pack of chicken tenderloins from the freezer. He'd drop them in marinade and let them thaw in it, then throw them on the barbecue later. There'd be enough for two if he happened to see Jena down at the beach.

Inviting her to join him would be a neighbourly thing to do—nothing more!

Stripping off his work-day clothes, he pulled on an old pair of swim shorts, grabbed a towel and headed for the beach. A good swim in the solitude of the lake would wash away the tension the day had generated. Perhaps Linda had done him a favour, forcing him to seek refuge out here.

But the lake wasn't all his this evening. There, cutting

through the water with efficient grace, her long hair hidden beneath a bright yellow cap, was Jena Carpenter.

A rush he hadn't felt since he couldn't remember when tightened sinews in his body.

'A lake that's five kilometres long and two k's wide should be big enough for both of you!' he told himself, but the words failed to convince.

He dived in anyway, and found the water didn't transmit her presence, though it seemed slightly stupid for two people to be keeping carefully to their 'own' bit of the lake.

He kicked leisurely towards her.

'Hi, neighbour.'

She greeted him with a wary look—enough to make him regret his hospitable impulses.

'Hi!'

'Am I intruding on your solitude? Would you prefer to swim alone?' Daft question, but his brain wasn't working too well—something to do with the mesmeric effects of long, slender legs treading water only a metre in front of him and a shapely body made, it seemed, for swimsuit ads moving in a sinuous manner above the legs. 'Actually, I came over to ask if you'd like to have dinner at my place. I'm just going to throw some chicken pieces on the barbecue and put a salad together.'

She gave him an even warier look. The trip out from town had been uncomfortable, though they'd both maintained polite façades. Surely this, he felt, would be taken as a declaration of a truce.

'I'm quite all right on my own, you know. I've got food, bedding, lights and plenty of books to read.'

'I realise that, but as we're neighbours…I didn't see any harm… '

He sounded half-witted—perhaps less than half. Was there such a thing as quarter-witted?

'I suppose I could come,' she said, hardly overwhelming him with delight.

'OK,' he found himself replying, although any sane man

would have taken the negativity of her reply as an insult and
promptly withdrawn the invitation.

Jena continued to tread water, wondering why she'd agreed,
however reluctantly.

Because it was polite and you need a lift to work tomorrow,
she told herself, but she knew it wasn't. Though, given she
found Noah Blacklock attractive and right now the last thing
she needed in her life was a man to complicate her plans, she
should have been avoiding contact at all costs.

'What time?'

He looked surprised.

'I don't think much about time out here. I usually start the
barbecue when I go back from my swim and it heats up while
I shower, then I cook and watch the sun go down.' He paused,
then added, 'Why don't you come straight from your swim?
The weather's warm but I can always lend you a shirt if you're
feeling cold.'

Jena found herself agreeing again—although it was the
thought of a shower which had seduced her. She'd brought
plenty of water—to drink. It hadn't occurred to her to work
out the logistics of bathing water, thinking there'd be some in
the tank Matt had mentioned—even if it wasn't drinkable. And
although the lake was fresh water, swimming didn't give quite
the same feel of cleanliness, particularly as she had no intention of polluting the pristine environment with soap.

Compared to a wash in a small basin of water, a shower
would be bliss!

Noah swam away while she was making excuses to herself.
Apparently he'd done his duty and was satisfied. She watched
his tanned, fit form slice effortlessly through the water and felt
again the physical reactions of her own body, betraying her
when she most needed it to be strong.

Though wanting a shower and wanting a man were very
different levels of betrayal!

She turned over and, looking up at the blue arc of the sky,
kicked her way back to shore. If she raced up to the house
and found some clothes to put on after a shower, would it
make her reason for accepting his invitation too obvious?

Probably.

Well, she had the long shirt she'd worn over her costume when she'd walked down to the beach. She'd put it back on after the shower—buttoned up, it would look like a dress.

She wrapped her towel around her body so the shirt didn't get wet, and walked along the beach, her feet digging into the soft sand, her legs heavy with a reluctance she didn't want to analyse.

Noah was still swimming so when she reached the place where a mown strip of grass indicated a track up to a dwelling she sat down and looked around. His towel was dropped about twenty feet away, a red and green blob on the fine white sand.

Before her, the lake stretched like a shimmering sheet of glass, blurred at the edges by the reflections of the she-oaks which grew in the sandy soil above the high-water mark. To the east, a line of sand dunes marked the division between the freshwater lake and the surf beach and ocean. To the west, the sun was already sinking behind the reed-thin leaves of the she-oaks, the beginnings of what promised to be a spectacular sunset already painting colour across the sky. Violet bled down into a dusky pink which teased its way through the range of reds towards vermilion on the horizon.

'I'm going for a jog before I go up to the house. Would you like to go ahead and use the shower?'

Jena had been so absorbed in watching the deepening colours in the west she hadn't heard Noah leave the water. He lifted the towel and rubbed it over his face and chest, though the water trickling down from his hair immediately wet his skin again.

'Clean towels in a cupboard just outside the shower room. I'm sure you'll find whatever you need.'

Mesmerised by a trio of droplets racing each other down the smooth tanned skin of his chest, Jena didn't reply—well, not immediately.

Neither did she protest that she couldn't use his shower. She'd already lost that battle with herself.

'Thanks,' she managed as he dropped the towel and turned

to jog away, denying her the opportunity of seeing which droplet won.

In the race to his waist—or the top of the faded swimsuit which had ridden on his lean hips?

She felt another blush—second rarity today—heat her cheeks, and scolded herself on her lack of control.

Commitment, that's what she needed. Hadn't she all but convinced Matt she had it by the bucketload? What she had to do now was get through these weeks in the shack and she'd land the one and only female spot in his new challenge survival series. Then she'd prove herself a capable and resilient woman—intelligent, too, as the challenge was mental as well as physical. She'd *make* people take her more seriously.

She walked up towards the small dwelling, and smiled when the clearing widened and she could see the little wooden structure. Although the design suggested Matt's place might have been built to the same plan, it was obvious what a little care and attention could achieve. The unpainted timber had weathered so it had a silvery sheen, against which the bright canvas deckchairs, set out in front of it, provided a vibrant contrast.

Wooden louvred doors had been concertinaed back so that outside and inside melded into an inviting living space. There were more canvas chairs in here and a couple of couches which, she suspected, could be turned into beds for extra guests.

Towards the back of the room, the right-hand corner became a small but functional kitchen, while on the left a door led into a hall which gave access to the bathroom.

No bedrooms?

Intrigued but uncomfortable about prying, Jena cautiously opened a door which she'd imagined led outside.

It did, but only onto another wide timber deck, roofed over but open on the sides—a combined sitting area and breezeway. Beyond the breezeway was a small, newer, two-storeyed structure, walls of louvred glass revealing a double bedroom upstairs and a weird assortment of double bunks and beach gear on the lower floor.

Smiling to herself as she imagined family holidays when all

the beds were occupied, she went back to the bathroom, showering swiftly so she'd be out before Noah returned.

Almost out!

She was delayed because of the shirt, which hadn't been such a good idea. She put it on as planned and buttoned it, then realised it was so sheer she might just as well have been naked. Back into the swimsuit—with the shirt as a cover-up.

He was on the front deck when she emerged, poking at the fire he had burning in the barbecue, so intent Jena had time to study his broad shoulders and tapering waist.

More like a lifeguard than a doctor—that was her immediate impression. Most doctors she'd met had little time for keeping fit and existed on a diet of fast food.

'You do eat chicken?' He must have sensed her presence for he turned to ask the question, but the sight of his face, dark hair still damp, the hard bones of cheek and jaw emphasised by the barely dry tautness of his skin, snatched at her breath and made answering impossible.

She nodded and looked beyond him to where the sunset was living up to its promise of bright beauty.

'Beautiful, isn't it?' she said quietly, hoping he'd think she was concentrating solely on nature's spectacular show.

'Very,' he said, but his eyes didn't turn towards the sunset and the husky timbre of the word made more than her cheeks heat.

CHAPTER FIVE

A FEW notes of a Bach suite made Jena turn towards the house, but Noah had obviously recognised the signature tune of his mobile because he abandoned the barbecue and strode past her.

Not wanting to eavesdrop, she took his place in front of the fire. The coals were beginning to glow through the grill plate but, knowing many men felt territorial about their barbecues, she refrained from poking it.

'Dinner's off, I'm afraid, although you could cook yourself a couple of pieces of chicken if you like,' he said, hopping out the door as he tried to pull on a pair of shorts over his bathers and shrug into a shirt at the same time. He paused to push his feet into casual canvas shoes.

'Crisis?' Jena asked, though a whiteness around his lips had already told her the answer.

'And then some,' Noah muttered grimly, his long legs eating up the space between house and car. 'You'll find your own way back to Matt's? The beach is safest.' He frowned at her.

'I'd suggest you wait but it could be an all-nighter.' He paused, then added, 'Some drunk holding his wife and kids hostage in a tent, would you believe? In the camping ground just up the road.'

Jena followed him towards the car, hoping to hear more details.

He turned again, frowning more fiercely this time.

'No! Hell! What am I thinking? Come on, get in the car.'

'Get in the car?'

'Well, it's obvious you can't stay here—or at Matt's place—with some madman loose with a gun. You'll have to come with me.'

And be about as welcome as a head-lice infestation, Jena

60

thought, but he was right, there was no alternative. No way was she braving the darkness on her own under these circumstances.

'Well, if there are kids involved you might need extra help,' she offered, more to answer the taunts of cowardice an inner voice was uttering than to appease Noah.

He couldn't have looked more surprised if the house had made the suggestion, but Jena didn't wait for a reply, walking around to the passenger side and climbing into the Jeep.

'I'll stay right out of the way,' she told him as he climbed in beside her, grumbling under his breath, no doubt about being stuck with the added responsibility of a woman. 'I've got enough sense to know an extra person can sometimes do more harm than good.'

The noise that greeted this remark could only be described as disbelieving, but he didn't reply, merely telling her to hang on as he was going to drive along the beach.

The powerful engine growled to life, and Noah, wondering if there wasn't a bit of gratitude mixed with his aggravation towards Jena Carpenter, guided it past the shack and down the mown strip to the beach. With kids involved, she *could* come in handy.

The sun had disappeared completely and the moon not yet risen, but the lake seemed to give off its own luminosity so he drove with only the parking lights, not wanting the brightness of full headlights to further upset the man at the camping ground.

'Do you know anything about him?' Jena asked.

Noah shook his head.

'The camping ground is within the national park so there are no people living there permanently, but a lot of the backpackers who come to town to earn a bit of travelling money, picking fruit or vegetables, set up their tents out here. They prefer it to the lodges in town.'

'So it's unlikely the family are alone in the park?'

'Most unlikely!' Noah said grimly. 'Though I imagine the police will clear the area as soon as they arrive.'

'As soon as they arrive?' his passenger repeated. 'They're not there?'

'Mac Talbot, the park ranger, phoned them first and then me. I'd say, even allowing for getting some clothes on, I'm still at least ten, maybe fifteen minutes ahead of them.'

The sound of shots suddenly rang through the air, unmistakable as being anything but gunfire, the noise itself a violent intrusion in so peaceful a place. His own nerves leapt and he sensed a tensing in his passenger, but she didn't scream or show any other indication of fear or hysteria.

He turned on his headlights now, and drove more swiftly, leaving the beach where a faint smudge of a track led beneath the low-hanging branches of a pandanus palm.

The scene at the park, lit by the headlights of a high-set four-wheel-drive utility, was like a surreal painting. One family-sized nylon tent, bravely blue and orange, was in the foreground while a scatter of smaller one- and two-man tents seemed to be shrinking away from it, as if trying to disappear into the bushes.

Shadowy figures moved on the fringes of the scene, and from the tent came the sound of a woman sobbing.

Noah pulled up beside the utility and leant out the window to speak to its driver.

'What's happening?'

'We don't know. The family have been here for three days—planning to stay on till Christmas. Mrs McDonald went to town today, left her husband with the kids. She came back about half an hour ago, went into the tent and the next thing we knew there's crying and screaming.'

The man rubbed his hand across his face.

'The young people were all coming back from work so I thought I'd better quieten things down. I went across and called out—not wanting to intrude by going into the tent—and he came out with a gun and told me to get the hell away, then went back inside.'

'And since then? The gunshots?'

Jena saw the man's shoulders lift and he raised his hands from the wheel in a helpless gesture.

'It was getting dark so after I phoned you and the police I thought I'd move the car a bit closer so I could call out to him—to them.'

Jena imagined the scene—the frightened ranger, anxious for the children, but not wanting to approach on foot.

'He didn't react to the car engine, but another car drove in about then and the headlights seemed to trigger something. That's when the shots rang out.'

'Someone might be injured in there,' Noah said. 'I'll have to get closer and ask.'

Jena curbed an urge to hold him back, while the ranger looked doubtful.

'Perhaps you should wait for the police…'

'By which time it could be too late,' Noah told him grimly. 'Don't worry, I won't take any unnecessary risks.'

He opened the door, and the click of the catch releasing, muted though it was, seemed to echo through the park.

'Be careful,' Jena whispered, and before he slid out into the night, he reached across and patted her hand.

'I will. I'm no hero.'

Then he vanished into darkness and Jena realised the ranger had turned off his headlights. Noah must have doused his as they drove up, for the camp site was nothing more than inky shadows.

As her eyes adjusted, though, she made out movement and realised Noah was approaching the tent from one side. When he was about twenty metres away, she heard his voice.

'Is everyone all right in there? I'm a doctor so please call out if you need help.'

A high-pitched wail greeted this request, rising so eerily into the night air that Jena found herself shivering. Lights and the hum of engines suggested more cars on the way. Police?

Or more unsuspecting campers returning to their tents?

Noah was moving closer, his voice audible although the words were indistinguishable, as if whatever he was saying was intended only for those inside the family's tent.

'He's going to go in,' Jena whispered, horrified to think he'd be so foolhardy but understanding his motives. The thought that a child might lie injured in there had her out of the car now, and was already propelling her feet towards the shadows.

'I'm coming in,' she heard him say, his voice steadily reassuring, but as he left the deeper shadows of the trees to move towards the front entrance of the tent the other cars arrived, their headlights once again illuminating the scene and throwing Noah's body into bright relief. The perfect target.

Jena stifled the scream which choked her throat, but the ranger must have given an order for the lights went out immediately, leaving not only darkness but no sign of Noah.

Then she heard his voice, coming from *inside* the tent.

'Hush now,' he was saying gently. 'Everything will be all right. You're sure none of you are hurt? Have you got a lamp, a torch? I'd like to check the children.'

Jena moved closer, walking in as a light came on and the woman said, 'He wouldn't have hurt us—not me or the children. He loves us. He was upset, that's all. He hadn't told us, see, and it was eating and eating away at him and today he had a few beers while I was in town and it all got too much for him.'

Noah was kneeling on the ground, one arm around the woman, while two blonde-headed little girls, their eyes wide with shock, nestled in her lap.

'He's gone,' Noah said to Jena. 'I suppose we should tell the police.'

But he didn't move and Jena, hearing more of the woman's rambling explanation about termination payments paying for the holiday, understood Noah's motives.

Left alone, the man might calm down, but if chased or hunted through the scrub, who knew what might happen?

The arrival of a tall policeman took the decision to tell or not tell out of their hands, but as both the children burst into tears at the sight of him, Noah motioned to Jena to take his place beside the woman. Rising to his feet, he led the policeman out of the tent.

While comforting the woman, Jena pieced together the story of the man who'd worked in the same factory for fifteen years then, two days before taking his Christmas leave, had been told he'd been made redundant.

'I didn't even know he had a gun,' the woman, whom Jena now knew as Rose, said. Looking around the spacious tent as she listened to the tale, Jena solved the mystery of the man's disappearance. As well as a hole in the tent-roof, where he'd obviously fired the gun in frustrated rage, there was a long rip from floor to roof in the rear wall.

'He did that with a knife,' Rose told her, and Jena shivered, thinking of the desperate man, alone in the darkness but armed with both a gun and a knife.

Noah reappeared.

'The police will need to talk to you,' he said, squatting down near Rose again, although the position must have been agonising for someone so tall. 'But I've suggested they do it at my place. It's just along the beach a little way and I've room for all of you. We'll leave a note here for your husband in case he comes back, explaining where you are.'

Noah indicated the torn nylon.

'You'll be eaten alive by mosquitoes if you stay here. He'll understand, and Jena, who's a nurse, will be there in case you or the children need anything.'

Jena raised a mental eyebrow at the job description, but understood Noah was underlining her presence in order to re-assure the woman. She'd have argued about the assumption that she'd spend the night at his place, only there was no way she'd be game to return to Matt's until the man was found. Which, for his sake as well as his family's, would hopefully be soon.

'Do you want me to write the note?' Noah's question, di-rected at Rose, brought Jena's mind back to the present. She watched the easy way he moved, leaning over to pick up a writing pad and coloured pencil one of the children must have been using earlier.

Rose nodded, and clasped the children more closely, then changed her mind.

'I'll do it,' she said, reaching out around the children for the notepad. The little ones snuggled closer to their mother.

Jena guessed their ages at about two and three. Would they remember this later? Would the short but potent drama played out in their presence come back to haunt them?

'All we can do is offer comfort and security,' Noah said quietly, while the woman wrote in big letters on the pad.

'Tell him it's the doctor's place, about four hundred metres east along the beach. Tell him I'll leave the front light on so he can find it easily.'

'I'll have to leave a light on here as well, so he sees the note,' Rose said, and Noah nodded and set the camping lamp with its long fluorescent tube down beside the note. He cleared clothes and towels from around it so it would be the first thing anyone entering the tent, either from the front or from the new rear entrance, would see.

Jena gathered up some clothes for the children, and found a cotton nightdress with a bear printed on it which she assumed was Rose's. She wrapped these in the towel, then found a small backpack and popped her collection into it, adding a small plastic-lined toothbrush bag containing soap and four toothbrushes.

'Do you need tablets or anything else for overnight?' she asked Rose, showing her what she'd already packed.

Rose passed the two children to Jena to cuddle and dived behind a small partition, returning with a pack of disposable nappies. She was obviously feeling better to be able to think of them.

'Let's go,' Noah said, and Jena lifted the older child while Rose picked up the little one. They followed Noah over to the Jeep where Jena helped strap all three of them into the back seat.

'You're inviting him to attack you,' the senior policeman warned Noah, when the family had been settled in his car and he was confirming arrangements for the authorities to interview the woman.

'I doubt he's dangerous. He'd been bottling up all his anger over his redundancy and something made him snap today. His wife thinks it might have been a letter she picked up at the post office. Maybe it's still in the tent.'

The policeman nodded, but he had enough sensitivity to wait until Noah had driven away before heading for the tent to check it out. As lights came on around the camp, Jena saw his silhouette as he slipped inside.

'We're having barbecued chicken for tea,' Noah remarked, though Jena knew from the way his eyes probed the darkness he was more concerned about the missing man than what they were about to eat. 'Do you like chicken?'

Silence from the back seat.

Jena turned to smile reassuringly at Rose but she, too, was scanning the dark bush outside the vehicle. She probably hadn't even heard the question. And although her arms held the two children tucked against her side, Jena knew her attention was focussed on her husband—and the dread his absence must be causing.

As they pulled up outside Noah's place, Jena slid out of the car and opened the back door to lift out one of the children.

'Wait here!' Noah whispered to her. 'I don't think he'd come into a house that's obviously occupied but I'd better check.'

'Check how?' Jena whispered right back. 'By walking in and waiting for him to blast you with his gun?'

Noah touched her arm, a gesture he doubtless meant to be reassuring.

All it did was string Jena's nerves tighter.

'I'll just turn on lights,' he told her. 'I've a master switch for the outside floodlights and the living-room light. It's in the shed, so when I come here late at night I don't have to fumble around in the dark.'

He moved away from her and seconds later soft light flooded the grass.

No sound came from the house—until Noah called from the verandah.

'Come on in. The fire's gone out but I'll cook inside.'

Jena lifted the child closest to her and settled the little one on her hip then, with her free hand, she snagged the bag she'd packed.

'Come on, Rose. Come inside. I'll fix you a hot drink—and something for the children. It must be nearly their bedtime.'

Jena waited for the woman to move, then walked with her to the house. Concerned about the children's unresponsive silence, she asked their names.

'The one you're carrying is Ruby and this one's Lily,' Rose told her, but when Jena said hello to Ruby, dropping a kiss on the little girl's blonde head, Rose laughed.

The harsh sound held absolutely no mirth and was so incongruous Jena was shocked. Then she saw the tears coursing down Rose's cheeks.

'She's deaf. They're both deaf,' the woman sobbed. 'They need so much, so many extra things, and then there's the money for the new cochlear implants—that's why Greg's so upset.'

Jena wondered how heavy a human heart could get as she drew Ruby closer, pressing more kisses on the child's soft skin—offering silent reassurance in the only way she knew.

They walked inside, Jena expecting to see Noah, but the living area was empty.

She felt a sense of loss, as if he'd deserted her to deal with her spiralling emotions alone.

'Look what I found.'

He appeared from the breezeway, a wicker hamper in his arms.

'Toys! My parents keep them here for grandchildren and other small visitors. Here!'

He set the basket in the middle of the floor and opened the lid, revealing a kaleidoscope of bright blue, red, green and yellow—the vivid colour mix of any number of toys thrown in on top of each other.

'If you watch the kids I'll get Rose helping in the kitchen,' he murmured to Jena, who had already pulled a soft clown doll from the basket and was waggling it temptingly in front of Ruby.

Rose set Lily down on the other side of the basket and once Ruby's chubby hands had taken hold of the clown, Jena found other toys to offer Lily.

The police arrived as they finished eating, and Jena offered to shower the children while Rose spoke to them.

Rose looked doubtful for a moment, then signed something to the little girls who both smiled as they looked at Jena. She held out her hands and they latched on, making her feel slightly less concerned about how much the drama had affected them.

Although who would ever know?

She realised the shower stall had obviously been set up with children in mind, with a hand-held spray which she could use to wet and rinse the little bodies. When she was done, she wrapped them in soft fluffy towels and held them close, wondering if the interview was over.

'I've got their nappies and some clothes,' she heard Rose say, and looked up to see the woman in the doorway.

The children immediately discarded their towels and flung their little naked bodies into their mother's arms. Sensing that the normality of readying the children for bed might be therapeutic, Jena let them go, staying behind to pick up the towels. She found a mop behind the door, and ran it over the floor to clean up the worst of the mess.

Though there was little she could do to dry herself. Her sodden shirt clung to her body, revealing the line and colour of the swimsuit she still had on underneath.

But the fine material did nothing to hide her nipples, puckered from the dampness, or the shape of her body, where the wet shirt clung.

'Damn!' she muttered at what she could see of her reflection in the small mirror.

'Not to worry, the policeman's gone. No one will see you.'

Noah's voice made her turn, and the look in his eyes as he took in her dishevelled appearance made a mockery of his 'no one' assertion.

It also made her shiver.

CHAPTER SIX

JENA followed Noah back to the living room, where the two couches had been turned into double beds and a swag, the great Australian invention of bedding packed in a water-resistant outer oilskin, was spread on the floor.

'I thought it might be more reassuring for Rose if we all bunked in together in the same room,' Noah explained. 'She's happy to share one of the beds with the children, and you can take the other. I'm used to the swag.'

Jena didn't bother protesting, knowing she wasn't likely to win—and not averse to a night on something softer than the old stretcher at Matt's. She'd have liked a change of clothes, a comb and a toothbrush, but she could hardly ask Noah to escort her home for such trivialities—for one thing, he couldn't leave Rose and the children—and there was no way she was facing the darkness on her own.

Rose settled the children into bed, then headed for the shower.

'Is she all right?' Jena asked Noah, when the woman was out of hearing.

'She's worried sick about her husband, and upset he didn't feel able to tell her about his job loss. I imagine they'd only just come to terms with having not one but two children born with a hearing impairment, now this on top of it.'

Jena shook her head, unable to imagine the emotional upheaval such knowledge must have caused the couple.

'Did she talk about the children's future? She mentioned implants earlier…'

Noah didn't answer immediately. Instead, he turned down the light in the living room then took Jena's arm and led her out onto the breezeway.

'I've got mosquito coils burning out here so it shouldn't be too uncomfortable to sit here for a while.'

The moon had risen, casting its silvery light over the bush, revealing the shape of chairs. Jena settled herself in one, and waited. She should have felt nervous, or at least on edge, with an armed man somewhere out there in the darkness, but somehow she couldn't believe the distraught husband and father would harm anyone, so all she felt was a little edgy about sharing the moonlight with Noah Blacklock.

Which was a reaction she'd have to give some thought to.

'Implants?' she prompted, to give her mind alternative thoughts right now.

'Apparently the older child is due to have an implant in the new year. It works by bypassing the damaged part of the ear, and children with an implant can hear a pin drop.'

'But is it enough to change them from hearing impaired to whatever counts as "normal"?' Jena asked.

'Normal?' he echoed. 'Yes, I often wonder what that is myself. However, as far as these children are concerned, the operation is only the start. I imagine that's what's worrying the family. The costs of the actual operation are usually borne by the state, but I've a feeling there's a lot more to it than the implant.'

'You don't know the half of it,' Rose said, coming quietly through the door and slipping into a vacant chair. 'Imagine the effect that hearing sounds for the first time can have on a child. They'll both need special programmes to teach them how to listen, and how to make sense of what they're hearing, how to interpret the sounds and how to develop speech.'

'Have you been signing to them from when you first found out?' Jena asked, and when she saw Noah's head turn in a reaction of surprise she chuckled. 'I saw Rose sign earlier and I've a friend who started signing to her baby when he was born, though he has no hearing impairment. It's apparently the trendy thing these days.'

'We've signed to them since we learnt there was a problem. Of course, we didn't know with Ruby, not until she was nine months old when enough strange things had happened to make us suspect. Then we had her tested and because what had caused her deafness was congenital, something she was born with, we had Lily tested far younger.'

'And once they've had the implants, you'll need programmes which integrate signing and speech?' Noah asked

'And need to spend a lot of one-on-one time with them.' Rose's sigh echoed in the darkness. 'At least with Greg at home, that should be easier.'

'But he'll get another job,' Jena protested. 'Someone who's worked for the same firm for fifteen years must have a good work record. He'll be snapped up.'

Was she being supportive, or plain naïve? Noah wondered. Or didn't she know about the unemployment situation?

'Where are you from?' he asked Rose, more to break the silence than for any other reason.

'We're from Brisbane,' she replied. 'Though we've talked often enough about moving to the country. We thought it might be better for the girls. Of course, there's no hope of moving for a while. They'll be hospitalised in the city and all the support services we'll need for them are down there.'

'It's a problem,' Noah agreed. 'For your family and for all people who need specialised help to get through illnesses or rehabilitation. At least while we still have some country hospitals operating, they can provide a base for visiting therapists and counsellors, and staff at the hospital can provide ongoing monitoring and support.'

'In a general way,' Rose said, her voice strained as she tried to pretend this was a normal conversation. 'Once the programmes have been set in place.'

There was a rustle in the bushes and they all tensed then laughed as a possum dropped from a tall tree beside the breezeway onto one of the beams above the deck.

'Wretched thing, frightening us like that!' Noah scolded it. 'But I guess I can find you a piece of fruit.'

As he left the deck to find a snack for the possum, Rose studied the little animal, sitting without fear above them, though its bright eyes were alert for any movement which might spell danger.

'We've seen them in the park,' she said. 'The ranger took us out at night and spotlighted the nocturnal animals for us.'

She was speaking softly, but her voice wavered at the end of the sentence, and Jena left her chair to kneel beside the distressed woman and put her arms around her.

'I'm sure your husband's OK,' she murmured. 'He needed to let off a bit of steam and now he's done it he's probably feeling more foolish than anything else.'

'But that's just the trouble,' Rose wailed. 'What if he feels so foolish he doesn't want to come out of hiding? He'd have seen the police arrive, and he must be frightened of what they'll do—whether they'll charge him.'

'I don't think they will,' Noah said, returning with slices of apple which he placed on the beam close to the possum. He was acting casually but Jena realised he was speaking quite loudly, perhaps hoping the absent Greg might be close enough to hear. 'After you explained the circumstances, Rose, I'm sure they saw it as an isolated incident that doesn't require any follow-up. They're making no attempt to find him—at least, not tonight.'

Was he right about the official reaction, or merely being reassuring? Jena wasn't certain but, then, she wasn't certain about anything that had happened on this strange day.

The talk became more general—about the lake, the national park and the holiday visitors.

'There are so many people from other countries camped near us,' Rose said. 'We were surprised but pleased the young people were seeing a different side of Australia. We thought they must be visiting all the national parks, until we learned they come to pick eggplants and capsicum.'

Noah chuckled.

'All kinds of vegetables,' he told her. 'Catering to the itinerant pickers has become a growth industry in the town. It's one of the reasons—'

He stopped suddenly and Jena wondered if he'd heard a noise but, even straining her ears she could hear nothing.

The possum, apparently satisfied with his snack, scampered

away, and Rose decided she'd check on the children—perhaps go to bed.

'I think we should all get some sleep,' Noah agreed, for all the world as if he hadn't left a sentence half-finished.

Well, he was the host, Jena reminded herself, and if he wasn't staying out on the deck, there was no way she intended lingering there, although there'd been a special ambience in the night air, as if the lightly lemon- and eucalypt-scented bush was promoting relaxation. Closeness.

She followed Rose inside, not wanting to be lured into considering closeness and Noah in the same thought. She pondered instead his half-finished sentence. She'd ask him about it tomorrow. It would give them something to talk about on the way to work.

Noah gave the women time to use the bathroom and do whatever women things the limited facilities would allow. Realising Jena had nothing to wear to bed—and not happy to think the beautiful woman might sleep naked so close to him—he crossed to the sleeping pavilion and dug through his old beach clothes, eventually coming up with a large T-shirt, soft from too many washes, which he felt might be comfortable night attire. Then he found some respectable boxer shorts for himself. Not a night for him to be sleeping nude either!

By the time he returned, Rose was in bed with the two children, and Jena was standing uncertainly in the middle of the room.

'I pinched some of your toothpaste and used my finger for a brush, but I don't fancy sleeping—'

She broke off and smiled her delight when he waved the T-shirt at her.

'Thank you!' she said, and obviously meant it. 'The shirt's hardly decent without my swimsuit underneath it and sleeping in it wouldn't be too comfortable.'

He left the room to give her privacy, though some testosterone thing tempted him to take a peek.

Not that he did, of course. It'd be a sad day he couldn't control his testosterone!

Or so he told himself, talking away in his head as he

brushed his teeth, stripped off his clothes and donned the boxer shorts.

He returned to find all his house guests tucked into bed, eyes closed either in sleep or in preparation for it. Though he doubted whether Rose would sleep. Her body must be concentrated on her husband, her nerves strung tight, her mind haunted by what might be happening.

And what about Jena Carpenter? If he felt wrung out after a particularly unusual day, how was she feeling?

His mind threw up more questions about Jena but he put it down to hormonal interference again and refused to give them brain space. Wondered about the little family under his roof instead.

Wondered, also, whether Lucy had been right about him becoming soft in the head—giving up a good job in the city, collecting 'lame ducks', as she'd called his young friends, and now taking in more strays.

Thinking about Lucy and her refusal to accompany him to Kareela was depressing. He'd been so certain he'd known her as well as any man could have known a woman, then he'd realised, when he'd mentioned his plans, he hadn't known her at all. Especially when she'd brought up the subject of a more open relationship, admitting she'd had the occasional affair during their time together. He shut her away in another corner of his mind—a different corner to the one where Jena lurked. He didn't want any confusion!

He thought about his new 'strays'.

Who did he know in the city who might give Greg a job? He'd worked as a maintenance man on machines in a factory.

But what kind of machines? The kind they had in hospitals?

Though big hospitals had all kinds of machines, from vehicle engines through to specialist equipment. He'd contact the maintenance manager at the Great Western and see what he could find out…

He smiled into the darkness.

He should have told Lucy it wasn't so much helping lame ducks as doing what he could for fellow human beings.

Which was, after all, a basic tenet of medical practice.

* * *

Soft noises from one of the children woke Jena, who sat up and looked around, surprised to find sunlight flooding the room. Rose was also awake, although one look at her pale face and darkly shadowed eyes suggested she hadn't slept well—if at all.

There was no sign of Noah, though his swag was still stretched out on the floor.

'I didn't hear him go. I must have fallen asleep just as the sun was coming up because I could see the sky lightening, and hear the birds, then I don't remember any more.'

'I'm sure things will work out all right,' Jena said, although she wasn't sure at all. 'Do you want to use the bathroom? I'll sit with the kids.'

Rose's answer was a tired smile which made Jena's throat tighten.

'You go first,' Rose insisted. 'That's the least I can offer after you and your boyfriend have been so good to us.'

Jena was about to deny the 'boyfriend' tag when she realised Rose had more to worry about than the relationship between two strangers. She slipped out of bed and hurried to the bathroom, using her finger again on her teeth and borrowing Noah Blacklock's brush to untangle her hair.

She kept his T-shirt on—it was far more comfortable than getting back into her swimming costume and shirt—and was in the kitchen, opening cupboard doors in search of breakfast cereal, when Noah returned.

Noah and a stranger who, from the way he greeted Rose and his children, must have been Greg.

Jena decided it was a good time to leave. With all the emotion in the air, no one would notice her absence.

'Sneaking away?'

Noah's voice halted her as she made her way around the side of the house.

She turned to see him standing on the back deck, seeming ten feet tall and very good-looking in his rough-hewn way.

'Definitely!' she said, then she grinned at him, hoping to defuse the beginnings of an inner reaction. 'Actually, I'm getting a lift to work and it wouldn't do to be late. From what I've seen of my chauffeur he's a bit testy in the mornings.'

Noah returned her smile, and Jena felt a dangerous fizz of excitement in her blood.

No way! she told herself. Not now when the job you want means you'll be away for months at a time. You know from experience what frequent absences do to a relationship.

'Drive you home.'

She'd missed the first bit but assumed it had been an offer. Not wanting to spend more time than absolutely necessary with the man, she held her arms out wide to embrace the bushland.

'On a glorious morning like this? No way! I'll walk back along the lake.'

He studied her for a moment, as if deciding whether to do the macho thing and insist, but Jena wasn't taking any chances.

'You've house guests!' she reminded him, then she waved and hurried away.

Noah watched her go, knowing she was right and he had to deal with his visitors, though they were of secondary importance in the decision-making process. Mainly, he should have let her go because not letting her go could cause problems.

Or exacerbate those already in existence.

Stupid to deny a physical attraction towards the woman when his body reacted every time he saw her—or even sensed her presence nearby. But he could ignore it. Wasn't being in control of one's body one of the advantages of maturity?

He sighed as he walked back into the house, hoping to find the reunion over so he didn't have to witness more emotional scenes. Listening to Greg's story when he'd found him in the torn tent had been as heart-wrenching as Noah could deal with in one morning.

The family was sitting on the couch, the parents arm-in-arm, the two children nestled between them.

'Why don't you stay here for the rest of your holiday?' he heard himself saying. 'I've been worrying about Jena being on her own in her friend's shack, so I'll bunk down over there.

I haven't been here long, so it will only take a few minutes for me to throw my stuff together, then I'll drive you back over to the camping ground, Greg, and you can pack up and drive back here in your own time.'

He hesitated, then put the obvious into words.

'You might feel more comfortable here, away from the park. You've a phone if you need it, and no one will be using the place until New Year's Eve when my sister and her family will arrive.'

Greg disentangled himself from his family and crossed the floor. He stopped a metre short of Noah, and put his hand out.

'I don't know who you really are, or why you're doing this, mate, but you won't regret it, and I won't forget it.'

They shook hands as if it were a deal they were sealing, then Noah excused himself.

He didn't know why he was doing it either. In fact, six months ago, if he'd heard himself making the offer, he'd have considered seeing a psychiatrist.

Or Lucy would have had him certified and saved him the trouble.

But that had been before the death of a young girl he'd barely known, a girl called Amy—

He switched off thoughts of Amy, Lucy and the past. He had to pack. Jena Carpenter wouldn't let him forget it if he happened to be late.

Jena Carpenter! Hell! He hadn't for a minute considered how she was likely to feel about his decision to share her accommodation.

His lips twitched into a smile. Now he thought about it, he was quite looking forward to seeing it!

'You can't stay here!'

Jena didn't yell or scream the words, throw a tantrum, or even, now he studied her more closely, seem unduly upset.

Just definite.

Very definite.

'I don't want to leave Greg and Rose without any back-up. Not for a day or two, anyway,' he explained.

'And?' she demanded, obviously not believing this weak excuse.

'I told the police I'd assume responsibility for them—for Greg, actually—if they didn't press charges against him for what happened. I can hardly go off to town and leave them out here.'

He peered into the blue eyes, hoping for a sign of understanding—of weakening.

No luck! They were as unyielding as sapphires—dark, glittering sapphires.

'If you're worried about your virtue…' he held up his hands in a surrender signal '…rest assured you'll be quite safe. I'm off women, if not for a century, at least for a decade or two.'

Ha! A reaction! The slight sardonic lifting of an eyebrow reduced his jokey remark to ashes.

'As if!' she muttered, in case he hadn't got the message.

Noah shifted uneasily. The bag was growing heavier and he was going to end up late for work. Perhaps if he tried another tack… After all, his family and Matt's had been friends, back when they'd all holidayed here.

'I realise it's not your place, but if I phone Matt—explain the situation to him…'

That got a reaction. She stepped towards the steps, missed falling through a hole in the floor by a millimetre and grasped his arm.

'Don't phone Matt!' She all but shrieked the words this time. 'Oh, don't do that. Stay here if you have to. I understand about the family, how they wouldn't want to go back to the camping ground, about responsibility and all…'

The words died away as if the implications bothered her, then she straightened and looked him in the eyes.

'But you can't tell anyone. None of the crew, and none of the staff at the hospital who might tell the crew. No one. It *has* to be a secret.'

The words had tumbled out in such an impassioned tone there was only one interpretation he could put on it. She did, as he'd first suspected, have some relationship going with Matt.

Yet his reaction wasn't the satisfying feeling of being right, but something more suggestive of disappointment. Which made no sense at all.

'Well, after that warm welcome, I guess I can drop my bag. I'll leave the swag in the car until tonight,' he said, stepping up onto the shaky verandah to deposit his canvas carryall on the floor just inside the door.

One brief glance was enough to tell Noah the exterior impression of the dwelling's deterioration was mirrored on the inside.

'It's got to be a penance of some kind,' he said, turning back to where Jena, still radiating tension, now waited at the bottom of the steps.

'Why couldn't you have stayed with them, with Greg and Rose? Especially if you've some kind of official responsibility?' she demanded. 'To just walk out and leave the family in your house is mad. You don't know them and only last night the man was running around in the dark with a gun and a knife.'

'He gave me the gun, an old air-rifle, and the knife was a small fruit-paring knife, hardly a deadly weapon.'

'It was still a quixotic decision!' Jena snapped. 'What are you? One of those angels who's only halfway to heaven, doing good deeds to wipe the slate clean of the bad you did before you died?' She glanced his way before adding, 'Must have been really bad!'

He shrugged uncomfortably, mainly because he didn't fully understand this new rash and impulsive person he'd become.

Quixotic was a kinder description than insane, which was what Lucy had called him when he'd made his first momentous decision towards lifestyle changes. And to be thought a halfway angel was infinitely better than to be considered a total fruitcake.

But Lucy wasn't the issue here. Greg and Rose were.

'Would you have sent them back to the camping ground after what happened? Imagine how embarrassed they'd feel. They'd pack up and go home for sure. And don't you think maybe they need a bit of a break before they have to face the realities that lie ahead of them?'

Noah followed her down the steps as he spoke, but knew from the set of her shoulders that, while she might agree, she still wasn't happy.

'You could have stayed with them,' she repeated, although the words lacked conviction this time. 'Why's a doctor living so far from work anyway?'

'You should be glad I am, or you'd be walking into town now!'

He snapped the words at her because getting into the car with her, smelling the faint fragrance which might simply be the soap she used, had made him realise just how stupid this idea really was.

It was going to put him into even closer contact with Jena Carpenter than the job would entail, and if sitting in a car with her brought his hormones into play, what would living with her do to them?

She's Matt's, he reminded himself, but somehow it didn't help. After all, Matt had stolen Bridget Somerton!

Funny! He could remember how he'd felt, remember vowing revenge, but couldn't remember the girl's face—or anything more about her, other than her name.

Couldn't even remember seeing Matt going about with her.

He'd probably been aggravated because Matt had always aggravated him—right from when they'd first met as youngsters and his mother had begun to hold Matt up as an example to him. 'Matt doesn't come home from fishing with his shorts all torn. Matt helps his mother with the dishes. Matt doesn't answer back.'

Matt the perfect!

The comments had seemed endless and had fuelled a natural antagonism between the two of them, so they'd alternately fought or avoided each other through six weeks of summer holidays every year of their childhood and adolescence.

'Well?' Jena demanded, as they drove towards the village. 'Why *are* you living out there? I'd like to know.'

'I lent my house in town to friends,' he said, actually

pleased to have a way to introduce his 'friends' into the conversation. Talking about Carla and co. would keep his mind off the scent of soap.

But a hoot of laughter from his passenger made him forget this aim, and he turned towards her.

'What's so damned funny about that?' He growled his irritation at her reaction.

'How many houses do you have?' she managed to ask, although laughter still hovered on her lips. 'How many more have you given away?'

She peered at him suspiciously, but the smile hovered on her lips and the tiny dimple flirted in her cheek. 'You're sure you're not an angel?'

Noah ignored the angel thing.

'I haven't given any away!' The words were just out when he realised they weren't entirely true. He had, in fact, given an old city house to the drug rehabilitation organisation. But it had only been a small house, an investment he'd bought while still a student and paid off by renting space to other students.

It had been in terrible condition—

'There *is* another one—isn't there?' his irritating passenger crowed. 'I can see from the look on your face.'

'That was different,' he protested. 'It didn't count and the house in Kareela and the lake house are both only lent on a temporary basis. My friends in town will be shifting into their own house as soon as some repairs are done. I came out here because I didn't want them to feel I was breathing down their necks—they're young, you see. And Greg and Rose are simply finishing their holidays at the lake.'

To his surprise, Jena seemed to accept this explanation, for her chuckling stopped.

He glanced towards her and caught a puzzled expression on her face and blue eyes scanning *his* face as if trying to read the answer to some mystery in it.

'What now?' he demanded, when the scrutiny began to unnerve him.

Her frown deepened and when she spoke it was slowly, as if she needed to test every word before it came out.

'You don't seem to be enjoying it. Getting any pleasure from this philanthropy. You're kind and generous and far more impulsive than anyone first meeting you would believe, but it doesn't seem to be fun.'

'Fun?' Noah echoed the word as if it was foreign to him and frowned right back at her. 'Why should it be fun?'

She shrugged.

'Perhaps not fun, but fulfilling in some way—pleasurable.'

'I think there's more to life than fun and pleasure,' he growled, then he turned his attention back to the road. 'Though perhaps in the make-believe world of television, that's a hard concept to master.'

The silence eventually made him glance her way again, but she was staring out of the window, although by now they were on the highway and the view was uninspiring.

'Perhaps you're right,' he heard her say. The words were little louder than a sigh.

She sounded so unlike the teasing passenger he'd had earlier that he wondered if he'd been too harsh, but it was too late to try to make amends. He had to slow as they came into Kareela, and keep more of his attention on the road and the schoolchildren riding bikes and scooters along the verge.

Jena was thinking of the words 'make-believe' and the condemnation Noah had fired at her yesterday—about Matt's challenges being entertainment, not reality. Yesterday she hadn't wanted to think about it because yesterday being the first female to undertake one of Matt's challenges had been terribly important to her. She knew most of the impetus behind this desire arose from not getting the job she'd really wanted, but life had been empty lately and lacking spark and she needed the new personal 'challenge' to prove something to herself.

So she didn't particularly want to consider the 'make-believe' aspect of television today either, because if she did she might have to rethink the new career path she'd chosen.

Which would make the entire exercise of staying out at Matt's place pointless.

Although, with Noah there, it was pretty pointless anyway.

Except Matt didn't—and hopefully wouldn't—know.

But wouldn't that be cheating?

Not when living with a schizophrenic, funless almost-angel might prove more of a challenge than any animal or insect infestation at the shack…

She sighed again just as Noah turned off the engine, so the sound hung in the air.

'Problems, Blondie?' Noah murmured, and the sympathy in his voice atoned for his use of the dreadful nickname.

'Just confused,' she confessed. 'So damn confused!' She spoke the truth, then added more truth. 'And it's all your fault!'

'My fault? What the hell have I done? Anyway, where confusion's concerned, you can join the club.' All sympathy was gone. He delivered the words then got out of the car and walked away, his long strides and erect carriage suggesting he was as anxious to escape from her presence as she was to be rid of him.

Because he'd made her reconsider the goals she'd so recently set for herself?

She thought about this, searching for an honest answer.

Not really, she decided, then refused to consider any alternatives. There were days when one could have too much honesty.

She'd begin the day again—first with a visit to Kate who would surely be released from hospital this morning.

Though later she'd have to see Noah again, and get acquainted with his schedule.

CHAPTER SEVEN

KATE was sitting on a chair by Mrs Nevins's bed, her hands full of the bright knitting Jena had seen but not examined.

'Look at it, Jena! It's more art than knitting—look at the colours and swirls of pattern.'

Kate, restricted by the lack of movement in her injured shoulder, pushed the bundle at Jena and instructed her to hold it up.

'It's just as beautiful on the back—or is there no back and front?' another voice remarked, and Jena turned to find a very thin young girl standing right behind her.

'I'm Carla,' the newcomer continued. 'I met Kate last night and we've been talking. She said she'd introduce us and I didn't want her to forget.'

Jena took the hand Carla offered, feeling bones as fragile as a bird's just beneath the skin.

'She's one of the kids living in Noah's house,' Mrs Nevins added, 'and there's a couple more girls there. She thought you might like to teach them modelling.'

The elderly woman looked Jena up and down, as if sizing up her aptitude for modelling—or the teaching of it—while Carla and Kate both looked embarrassed.

'I was going to tell you—' Kate began, while Carla also hastened into words.

'It's not modelling, but I was going to ask—'

Jena patted her shoulder.

'We'll talk about it later. First I'd better see the crew, shoot any trouble, as trouble-shooting's in my job description, then I'll come back. You'll be here?' she added to Carla.

'I'm getting out as soon as I've seen Noah, but he'll tell you where I live—well, where I'm staying for the moment. Or I could wait…'

'I'll be upstairs shortly,' Kate told her. 'I've stayed the

85

night, which is all the doctor wanted. I'll be careful of my shoulder, but I want to work.'

So you can stay in Kareela with John, Jena guessed, but she said nothing, understanding how poor Kate must feel.

As she walked away, she wondered about the advisability of keeping the injured woman on location—about workplace health and safety, not to mention compensation ramifications. She knew if Matt was there, Kate would be on her way home the moment she was released.

But Matt wasn't there.

Or likely to be. It wouldn't occur to him to check up on her out at the shack—he trusted her.

Wasn't she betraying that trust by letting Noah stay?

'Of course, but only briefly!' She said the words aloud, to reassure herself, but her conscience wasn't entirely eased.

Noah was also thinking about Matt Ryan. Gossip had it that Matt was the perennial bachelor—a man determined to live life to the full, but on his own terms, unhindered by the demands of a wife or family. He might be seen with beautiful women everywhere he went, but marriage? As far as Noah knew, it was so far down Matt's list it was off the planet.

Yet Jena must think he was serious about her, or having Noah sharing the house wouldn't have sent her into such a tizz.

He signed the pile of letters Peta had left on his desk, checked his diary and groaned. Meeting day! Though he had time to go around the wards first. Carla would be waiting to go home.

Home?

Would she, or any of them, ever think of Kareela as home?

He amended the thought to 'Carla will be waiting to be discharged' and walked out of his office, crossing the foyer in time to see long slim legs, fast becoming familiar, disappearing up the stairs.

He was mad to even consider living at Matt's place.

But if he shifted back to town, knowing she was alone out there... Or the McDonalds might need help...

'Happy meeting day!' Rhoda teased him, when he entered

the women's ward first. As the senior nursing sister she was the official DON, Director of Nursing, although in a small hospital where financial considerations meant she had to do the same hands-on nursing hours as the rest of the staff, it simply meant more paperwork.

And the added irritation of meeting days.

He flicked through a pile of notes on the desk and was about to begin when Jena appeared.

'I'm following you around for a few days, remember?' she said, and although she spoke lightly, he fancied he heard strain in her voice, though why he should be giving *her* problems, he couldn't fathom.

'Mrs Burns isn't responding to the antibiotics the pathology lab suggested.' Rhoda had smiled at Jena then got down to business, handing Noah a file and pointing to the relevant entry.

'Is the infection still only in her throat? No sign of it in her knee?'

'Yes and no, but she's feeling so ill she doesn't want to continue the exercise she should be doing. It's knocking her about, Noah.'

'And could still go to her knee,' Noah muttered as he read the pathology report on the latest throat swab he'd taken from Mrs Burns. 'Let's see her first.'

He left the ward, heading for the private rooms. Not wanting to spread contamination through the hospital, he'd isolated this patient and ordered extra precautions be put in place to prevent the spread of bacteria.

But as he moved, although his mind was fixed firmly on work, his back tingled with an awareness of Jena's presence.

Something he'd have to get over if he was to survive the next few weeks!

'Why aren't the antibiotics working?' Mrs Burns asked, as Noah entered, giving him no time to introduce the visitor. Out of the corner of his eye, he saw Jena prop herself against the wall, keeping tactfully out of the way as Rhoda joined him by the bed.

'Because the strain of staph infection you picked up is a

persistent little beastie and we might have to try three or four antibiotics or a combination of more than one to knock him out.'

'Soon?' his patient said hopefully.

'Soon!' he promised, but he wasn't nearly as sure as he sounded.

He examined Mrs Burns, checking her heart particularly as endocarditis, a condition affecting the lining and valves of the heart, was one of the complications of staph infections. Then he checked her lungs, as she'd originally been hospitalised this time for pneumonia—the throat infection having been a later discovery.

'Well, apart from your throat, you seem to be doing well,' he told her when he'd finished.

'Apart from my throat, I'd be able to eat,' she retorted. 'You've no idea what it's like—this awful taste, and the smell in my nostrils.'

Noah offered genuine sympathy. He'd seen enough infected wounds for the smell to be all too familiar.

'Well, we've tried the vancomycin and it didn't work, so we'll move on to rifampicin and possibly gentamicin. The problem is that your staphylococcal infection is different to the more common hospital staph, so it's a matter of trying all the things which have worked before on other people, knowing we'll eventually find a combination to knock it on the head.'

'Being in hospital, we can keep you on fluids and special drinks with enough nutritional content to keep your body healthy, so not eating shouldn't be a problem,' Rhoda added. 'Although you should keep trying to eat what you can.'

'And you have to exercise,' Noah reminded their patient. 'The physio will be here tomorrow and she'll tear strips off us if she thinks we've been letting you lie around all day.'

Mrs Burns frowned at him, but promised to try to do more.

'I'll send one of aides in to walk with you as soon as they finish on the wards,' Rhoda promised.

As they walked away, Jena falling in quietly behind them, Rhoda turned to Noah.

'Will we beat it?' she asked. 'Or have some of these strains become so resistant to antibiotics there's nothing strong enough to combat them?'

He grinned at her.

'Defeatist! Of course we'll beat it. We'll start on the new drugs today and if they don't work we'll take another swab and ask for more suggestions. The bacteria the lab has isolated is more common on the site of central IV catheters or as a skin infection. In those cases the infected tissue can often be cut out—'

'But you can hardly cut out her throat!' Jena murmured, although he hadn't needed the reminder of her presence. 'How do you think it occurred?'

'Most likely from the tube inserted during the operation. It invariably causes irritation to the lining of the throat and provides an ideal place for the bacteria to thrive.'

'And the eating thing?' Rhoda asked. 'I've been giving her special protein-laden drinks and she seems able to tolerate them, but should we be watching her weight to make sure she's not becoming anorexic?'

'Good idea,' Noah agreed, pausing in the hall as he mentally listed alternatives for Mrs Burns.

They reached the men's ward and Rhoda walked him around the public patients. Once again, he was aware of Jena in their little group—even acutely aware of her—but that was his fault, not hers. Apart from one remark and a question, she'd been as unobtrusive as five-ten of beautiful shapely blonde could possibly be!

Colin Craig first. He was recovering from a car accident which had resulted in multiple injuries to his legs and ankles.

'So, how's the bionic man?' Noah asked him.

Colin was sitting up in bed, both legs in plaster—the left from below the knee, the right from above it.

'Cranky!' Colin told him, though failing to make eye contact as he watched Jena over Noah's shoulder. 'I thought the specialist said I could walk after a fortnight.'

'That's if everything looked good on the X-ray,' Noah reminded him. 'The screws and pins holding most of your shattered bones together allow new bone growth, and it's this, not the pins and screws, that will eventually mend everything. If you put weight on your ankles and legs too soon, this new bone is put under stress and anything under stress can break.'

'And your specialist said two to four weeks—not just two,' Rhoda reminded him. 'I know because I was there.'

Noah had to chuckle. Colin was Rhoda's nephew but, though she adored him and had gone to Brisbane every day while he'd been hospitalised down there, he wouldn't get any special treatment in 'her' hospital.

'I'll X-ray you again on Friday,' he promised Colin. 'So hang in until then.'

The young man didn't look at all appeased, although when an aide appeared with a wheelchair he brightened considerably.

'I'm going to mosey on out to the hall and see the television people come and go,' he explained.

'Not today, you won't,' Noah told him. 'Some of the crew have come to set up, but the chap who's narrating the series won't be here until next week.'

'That won't worry Colin. What he actually means is he's going to hang about in the hall to watch Jena here go up and down the stairs,' Rhoda explained. 'Most of the male staff are finding an excuse to be in the hall as often as possible.'

Noah glanced at Jena who'd gone a very fetching shade of pink.

'That's not true and you shouldn't tease him,' Jena objected, then she turned away, crossing the airy room to where Toby was sitting up in bed, watching the proceedings.

Colin, who'd blushed a fiery red at this defence, watched her go, and Noah realised Rhoda's comments were probably true.

'Well, at least the lad's got taste!' he said, feeling he might relieve the tension with a kind of man-to-man bonding comment.

Then regretted his flippancy when Rhoda raised her eyebrows and murmured, 'Not you, too? I thought you were off women for life.'

Noah ignored her, moving resolutely on to the next patient,

an older man who had recently been diagnosed with rheumatoid arthritis. Noah was working with a specialist in Brisbane to find a drug regimen which might provide relief for his pain.

And young Toby, where Jena waited, was next. He, too, was an arthritis sufferer, although hopefully his would only last through childhood. Noah hoped, with the latest treatments, Toby wouldn't carry too many crippling after-effects into adulthood.

'So, how's the lad?' he asked Toby, who managed a wan smile and asked his usual morning question.

'When can I go home?'

'Tomorrow, all being well,' he promised.

Toby accepted this verdict. He'd had enough flare-ups of the disease, when the pain became unbearable, to know he had to put up with these hospital stays.

This time, Noah was trying a different drug, one so new it had just come on the market. As they moved on, he explained to Jena why he'd kept Toby in hospital, wanting to monitor the lad's kidney and liver function for the first few days he was on it.

'And how's it going?' she asked.

'So far, so good,' he said.

'Will he suffer all his life?' Jena asked, and he heard very real empathy in her voice.

'Hopefully not,' he said, then, noticing the way Toby was still watching their visitor, he added, 'Would you like to sit with him a while? I'm only doing the same thing I've done with the others, checking on how they feel and what results we're getting from treatment. Seen one ward round, you've seen them all.'

He made a joke of it but, in fact, he'd be glad to be free of her presence for a short time. He'd heard of people suffering an instant attraction to someone of the opposite sex, but he wasn't that kind of person. It was Rhoda's fault with her sneaky 'not you, too' remark!

'Come on!' he said gruffly to the nurse in question, when

Jena had taken his advice and settled into the visitor's chair by Toby's bed. 'Let's get on with it!'

By the time he'd finished the round, and discharged Carla with a warning to stay out of fights, Jena was gone and he was running late for Jeff's meeting. Which would give the man another reason to complain.

He crossed the foyer and walked into the big office where two typists and a receptionist all pointed to their watches and shook their heads.

'Rhoda's later than I am!' he told them.

'Not good enough!' Peta whispered, but at that moment the door opened and the women all turned away immediately, bending their heads to give an impression of total absorption in whatever they were doing.

'You're late,' Jeff told him, and Noah sighed. He'd told himself he was going to stop arguing with Jeff, which meant he had to stop defending himself.

'I'm sorry to keep you waiting,' he said, hoping humility might get things off on a better footing.

'Well, Rhoda's still not here, but I wanted to get through the basics early because I've asked Jena Carpenter to join us. I think it's important we know the television crew's programme well in advance so we can make our arrangements accordingly.'

The statement was typical of the meaningless nothings that Jeff often uttered and which irritated Noah unbearably. Bureaucrat-speak, he called it. Hearing it now, he felt a muscle in his cheek begin to twitch, so he closed his eyes and counted silently to ten. Patience—that's what he needed.

A double dose if Jena Carpenter was going to be present.

'What have you done to so antagonise that man?' Jena asked, following Noah, uninvited, into his office at the end of the meeting. 'And don't bother telling me it's none of my business, because if I have to sit through that kind of tension on a weekly basis while I'm here, I think I deserve to have a little background on who's knifing whom and why.'

She shut the door and leaned against it, a posture that made much of the breasts he kept trying not to notice.

'We don't get on,' he said, more irritated by his inability to control his wandering eyes than by the question.

'Duh!' she muttered, and smacked her forehead. 'That much I'd gathered. I may be blonde, Dr Blacklock, but I'm not brain-dead.'

He had to smile, though he felt more like growling, but Jeff's meetings always produced a similar reaction.

Sensing his visitor had no intention of leaving without an explanation, and needing her out of the room before he could possibly think about work, he began a carefully edited version of the problem.

'Jeff didn't want a doctor here but the Health Department advertised anyway—'

'Hey, back up!' Jena said, raising her arms so her breasts shifted again—not that he was looking. She loped forward to sit down in his only spare chair. 'It's a hospital. Don't all hospitals have doctors? Can you have a hospital without one? Isn't there a contradiction there somewhere?'

He grinned at the perceptions she shared with most lay people.

'A lot of country hospitals no longer have doctors appointed as medical superintendents—that's the title given to the chief medical officer at a hospital, who is an employee of the state government and paid by them. Nowadays, smaller hospitals have local GPs, either paid as visiting doctors, doing the casualty and outpatient work on a roster system, or not officially connected at all, simply using the hospital for their own private patients.'

'So there's no doctor like you in these places, but when a GP puts a patient into hospital, he or she is responsible for that person?'

'Exactly,' Noah replied, though his attention had been distracted again—not by breasts this time but by the intensity of her blue eyes. Was she so interested in learning about this, or was it a trick of the trade?

'But where does Jeff come in? And why did your appointment annoy him? Surely it's easier to run a hospital if you've got a doctor?'

Noah gave a huff of laughter.

'You'd think so, wouldn't you? Actually, in hospitals where there's no doctor, the administrator, or chief executive officer as they call them these days, is the boss. He controls all the finances, allocates hours to visiting GPs, reports to the board and generally runs the place. The director of nursing, naturally, has a say, but as she usually works full-time at nursing as well, she's more than happy to leave a lot of the paperwork to the CEO.'

'And you coming here—having any doctor here—lessens Jeff's power? Is that what you're saying? But surely it's good for the town and the hospital itself.'

'You'd think so,' Noah said, and Jena heard the dryness in his voice and wondered just how deep the divisions went between the CEO and the doctor.

'But if he's ambitious—and if he wasn't he wouldn't care—wouldn't he want the hospital to be the best it can be? So he can prove his capabilities? Isn't he better off working *with* you rather than antagonising you?'

She leaned forward as she asked the question, puzzling over this seemingly petty division between the two men. But Noah didn't reply, merely closing his eyes as if praying for patience.

Because she was asking stupid questions and he was busy?

'I'm sorry.' She stood up and backed towards the door. 'It's a dreadful habit, this wanting to get to the bottom of things. My entire family complains about it. In fact, ''Jena, don't go on and on'' is probably the most commonly heard comment at family gatherings.'

She reached the door, muttered another apology and slunk out, scolding herself all the way. As if Noah Blacklock didn't have enough to put up with.

'Hi, there! I've been hoping to catch you.'

Jena reached the foyer and found Carla sitting on the bottom step, chatting to Colin.

'Off you go, Colin,' Carla told the man. 'This is going to be a private conversation.'

'In the hall, with people walking past all the time?' he said, but with a shy smile at Jena he wheeled himself away.

'Did Noah talk to you about this? I mentioned it to him yesterday,' Carla said.

Jena remembered Noah's almost schizophrenic change of attitude from grump to close to friendly the previous morning. Now she had the answer. The man had wanted something.

Hiding a niggle of annoyance, she said cautiously, 'I don't think he mentioned anything specific, but Mrs Nevins said modelling.'

'Not so much modelling as movement. I wondered if you'd teach us some movement. I know fashion parades are choreographed. Do you know any of that stuff? Choreography? Is there a science of movement? Things you do and don't do?'

The questions were so unexpected it took a moment for Jena to take it in.

'Who's "us"?' she asked, deciding to get down to basics while she thought about the rest.

'Noah's druggies. I thought you'd have known. You see, we want to give something back to the town, and thought we'd do a float in their Christmas street parade and kind of dance or do movement on it. Although it was Noah who worked out Kareela would be ideal, the town still had to accept us—which they've more or less done.'

'I'm sorry I asked,' Jena muttered. 'I'm more confused than ever. Start with Noah's druggies. What a bizarre phrase. Explain it for me.'

'It's what the town calls us,' Carla said, stepping forward and rolling up her sleeves to show ridged scars on the inner surface of her arm. 'Noah set up a halfway house for people who'd been through a drug rehab programme but weren't quite ready to face the world alone.'

'Here in Kareela? Is there a big enough drug problem in a small country town to warrant rehab and halfway houses?'

Carla laughed, and indicated the step. They both sat down.

'The rehab place is in Brisbane, and choosing Kareela for a halfway house was Noah's idea because it's close enough to the city for us to have friends or family visit—when we're first in a programme we don't get to see anyone—and also it's a big centre for backpackers.'

'I suppose that makes sense to someone,' Jena said, shaking her head and wondering if, despite her continued protestations, being blonde did alter one's thought processes.

'Noah's idea again, the backpackers,' Carla elaborated. 'He reckoned if we mixed and worked with people of a similar age who had their lives together, it would be inspiring for us.'

Light bulbs began to click on in Jena's head. She could imagine that the excitement generated among travellers from various nations could be inspiring to young people who, for a long time, had had no positive goals.

'And are you working with these people? Has the idea proved successful?'

Carla nodded.

'As far as I'm concerned, it has. I've had nothing for so long—no ambition, and no hope. Nothing beyond how to get the next hit. Since we've been up here we've been picking beans, and it's dreadful work. You're bent over all the time and the sun beats down on your neck, but at lunchtime you sit under a shady tree and hear all the different accents, and people talking about the mountains they've climbed in South America, the rapids they've ridden in India.'

She paused, then smoothed her shirt over her scarred arms.

'It makes you want to stay alive,' she said quietly.

Jena touched her shoulder.

'I've got to get back to my real job,' she said, 'but I'd be happy to do anything I can to help. Can I visit you when I finish here? After five? Give me your address and a few directions—I don't know the town at all.'

'I'll write it all down and leave it at Reception,' Carla promised, then she leant over and kissed Jena on the cheek. 'Thank you.'

Jena carried the thanks and impulsive gesture up the stairs with her. She had no idea what she could do to help the group with their 'giving something back' to the town, but she'd do her best to make their effort special. Though she'd have to make sure her car was drivable. She didn't want Noah to have to hang around waiting to give her a lift.

Thinking of Noah, she realised this was another 'angel' thing on his part. Not that she believed in angels, but as a man he'd risen in her estimation. Though why he'd allied himself with such a controversial group as drug addicts, or risked contention by introducing a number of them into a country town, she had no idea.

Perhaps a family problem—a close encounter of a personal kind?

The thoughts intrigued her, but she had no time to pursue them. Andrew was waiting at the top of the stairs, and the look on his face suggested more trouble.

'The hoist's not working. We've got the mock office and theatre all chalked out on the floor and the timber and furniture will be here tomorrow, but we can't get the darned thing going.'

'It's the ghost,' Kate said, and Jena frowned at her.

'Mention the ghost once more, especially to the rest of the crew when they arrive, and you'll be going straight back to Brisbane.' She turned to Andrew.

'Is it a hire hoist or one of our own? If it's hired, get onto the firm and get them to deliver another one. If it belongs to the company and they can't replace it, hire one.'

Andrew looked relieved and Jena realised it wasn't so much the hoist bothering him as taking responsibility for decisions. He went off to phone someone, herding the others downstairs to check on the props they hadn't lifted, leaving Jena on her own.

She crossed the open space that had once been a ward to where chalk marks and small red pegs showed where the 'office' would be built.

'Is this it?'

Noah's voice startled her. She'd heard footsteps but had assumed one of the crew was returning.

'Would that my real office was so big.'

'They need space to get the cameras in—one set up in front and one behind you, probably. I don't understand all the technicalities of it, but they seem to need any number of different angles to make things look real.'

Jena watched him pace within the chalk marks.

'Hard to know what's real sometimes. Do you find that?'

The question puzzled her because she sensed he meant something beyond the actual words, but second-guessing what Noah Blacklock might be thinking was impossible so she went with the literal interpretation.

'In this crazy entertainment business, so little is real it's best not to believe any of it.'

She waited for a reply, a comment, but he continued to pace, and when the silence began to fidget along her nerves she added, 'Did you want me?'

There was the slightest of hesitations—long enough to make her regret the phrasing of the question—but when Noah spoke he gave no indication he'd taken it any way but the way she'd meant it.

'I wondered if you'd spoken to the mechanic about your car. As I've forced my presence on you at Matt's place, the least I can do is provide transport, but I have a meeting with one of the therapists after work tonight and won't be heading out to the lake until late, possibly not until after seven.'

'After seven would suit me,' Jena told him, remembering her promise to Carla. 'Though I'll probably have my car back. You don't have to drive me.'

'Seems silly to be taking two cars back and forth over the track,' he said, but once again she sensed something more behind the words.

Moving in with her, wanting to drive her—was Noah keeping an eye on her for some reason? She studied him as he stopped pacing to peer out of the window. Straight-backed. Intense.

Attractive.

She felt a shiver beneath her skin and glanced around—wondering if perhaps the ghost had passed by her.

Though she didn't believe in ghosts any more than she believed in angels!

Or instant attraction.

'But if you have a late meeting,' she began, then felt the words falter on her lips as he turned towards her. He was silhouetted against the glass, a shadowy figure.

A stranger.

Yet somehow familiar.

'I'll let you know about the car,' she said, and he walked away, his tread heavy on the steps.

CHAPTER EIGHT

NOAH was nowhere in sight when Jena, satisfied that a new
hoist had been found and work could continue the following
day, was finally ready to leave the hospital. The receptionist
had gone, but an older woman was manning the front desk.

'A note for you? Carpenter?' she said, looking vaguely
around.

'Carla, one of the patients, was going to leave it,' Jena explained. 'With directions how to get to the house where she's
living.'

'Oh, Noah's house,' the woman said. 'I'll tell you where it
is.'

'Is it close enough to walk?' Jena asked, anxious about distance as the mechanic hadn't finished with her car though he'd
promised to deliver it to the hospital by six-thirty at the latest.

'No distance at all,' the woman said.

She proceeded to explain, the directions so good that Jena
found her way without needing the note, which had turned up
under the telephone directory.

She smiled to herself as she saw the house. Not exactly the
home she'd have expected a bachelor doctor to inhabit, but
ideal for a group of young people. Set on a huge block, it
nestled back amid trees and shrubs, wide verandahs stretching
across the front and down each side. Behind, Jena could see
the high fence of a tennis court, while to one side the blue of
a pool beckoned invitingly.

Carla greeted her at the front door.

'I'm the only one at home. The others aren't back from
work yet. Come on in.'

She led Jena through a wide hall with bedrooms off each
side and into a huge room which obviously ran the width of
the house. It was a combination sitting and dining room, with
a kitchen separated off by a high bar. Cane stools, their cush-

ions covered with a teal and terracotta print, lined the bar while
similarly covered cane armchairs nestled in a group at the far
end of the room.

In between was a dining table, cane-based and glass-topped,
the chairs echoing the prints with covers of either terracotta
or teal.

Jena felt a woman's presence in the colour scheme, and the
question of Noah's marital status occurred to her again.

Perhaps he was separated.

'We know we're only here temporarily so we're trying to
keep the place as clean and tidy as possible,' Carla said, ush-
ering her through the room and out to a back verandah, where
a barbecue area had been built beside the tennis court. 'Great
house, isn't it? It's nearly as good an inspiration for me as
meeting the backpackers. This is where I'm headed. I want a
house like this.'

Jena looked around.

'I think it would be more affordable in a country town than
a similar property in the city.'

Carla grinned at her.

'Then I guess I'll have to get used to living in the country.'

They settled on casual canvas chairs grouped together under
a gazebo and Jena, more to take her mind off the zillion questions about Noah this house had thrown up, spoke first.

'OK. Tell me what you plan to do—what ideas you've had
already.'

Now Carla looked hesitant.

'If only we knew!' she sighed. 'Seems we can't agree on
anything—well, not so much not agree as every time someone
has an idea we all leap on it and forget the previous one, so
all we're getting is confused.'

'What actually happens on the day?' Jena asked.

'They have a parade. Bob, who organises the work teams
and drives the bus to take us out to the various farms, told us
about it. It's the Saturday before Christmas. The parade starts
near the public library, goes down the main street, past the
shops and ends up in the park where there's a bit of a fair

with stalls selling food, dodgem cars and merry-go-rounds for the kids—that kind of thing.'

'You mentioned a float,' Jena prompted when nothing more seemed to be forthcoming. 'Are you going to make one?'

Carla sighed again.

'We thought about it, but none of us know the first thing about building anything and Bob pointed out we'd need a vehicle of some kind to go under a float and propel it along, so then we thought—you know how parades have clowns and things dancing along beside the floats? We thought we might do that.'

Jena knew exactly what they meant and could picture people in costumes accompanying floats in other parades. She had a vehicle they could use and, no doubt, the carpenters could knock up a float...

'The next idea was that, instead of dancing, we might do something in the park at the end of the parade. Someone suggested statues. Have you seen those buskers who pretend to be statues? They're usually painted gold or silver and they stand very still, but occasionally change position and people look at them for ages. We thought maybe no one had done that kind of thing in Kareela.'

Great! Jena thought. This girl thinks I can choreograph statues!

'I wouldn't have asked, only Kate said you'd travelled overseas a lot and I thought you might have some good ideas.'

'Let me think about it,' Jena said. 'What if I call in again—say, the day after tomorrow? Will you be here or will you be back at work?'

Carla touched the dressing just above her temple.

'No work for four days—doctor's orders,' she said. 'I'll be here.'

Jena said goodbye and was pleased when Carla suggested they walk out past the pool. What she'd seen of the house had been so appealing she wanted to see more.

The pool didn't disappoint her, nestled like it belonged in its sandstone surrounds, bright-leaved plants around it giving it the appearance of a tropical haven.

'Beautiful, isn't it?' Carla said, echoing Jena's thoughts.

'Very,' Jena agreed, more certain than ever that Noah had either bought this place with a woman or for a woman.

So where was she?

Had she died?

A recent bereavement might explain his quixotic behaviour—the mixture of kindness and anger.

Possible reasons for Noah's behaviour occupied her on the walk back to the hospital, although by the time she reached the car park consideration of his behaviour had taken second place to a review of his physical attributes—and why her body should find them so attractive.

Her vehicle was there, parked in front of the hospital.

She found the keys, and a bill for the repairs, under the front seat as promised, so she got in and drove out of the public car park and around to the staff area, parking beside Noah's Jeep. The pristine condition of his vehicle made hers, borrowed from her brother for this sojourn in the bush, look ready for the scrapyard.

So what, she told herself as she scribbled a note to tell him she'd gone back to the lake. At least having independent means of transport lessened the time she had to spend in his company.

Leaning across the bonnet of the Jeep to secure the note under a windshield wiper, she was thinking of the man who owned it and why attraction worked the way it did when his voice startled her so badly she actually leapt in the air.

'Pinching my windshield wipers?' he asked.

Jena pressed her hand to her heart, telling herself it was fright causing the rapid pulsing.

'Leaving you a note,' she managed to reply, though the quavery note in her voice was a dead give-away.

'To tell me you don't require a lift?' he queried, his eyebrows rising with his voice.

'Well, I don't,' Jena replied, her voice stronger now. 'As you see, I have my car and I'm ready to leave now, whereas you won't be going until after seven, I think you said.'

Then, to set some rules between them if this living together thing really *was* going to happen, she continued, 'And as you fed me last night, I'll return the favour tonight, but I assume you'll have your own supplies over at the house—enough for the couple of days you need to stay. As you noticed, I've limited storage space so I tend to shop every second day—just buying what I'll need.'

He grinned at her.

'BYO food, in fact.' The smile broadened, and even twinkled in his eyes, which, as far as Jena could remember, were usually either cool or appraising.

Twinkling, they were mesmeric.

'Plenty in both fridge and freezer and as I'll want to check on Greg and Rose this evening I'll bring some supplies back with me from there. I've a small portable fridge that runs on gas so I won't be taking up space in yours.'

Jena managed to get her mind off his eyes in time to catch most of the conversation. However, she couldn't produce much in way of a reply so she said, 'Good!' Which, she realised, made her sound totally inhospitable.

Unable to think of a way to redeem things, she added, 'Well, I'll see you later.' And climbed into the LandCruiser.

'But I'm on my way. The meeting finished early.'

Once again, Noah was preventing her from closing a car door. He was standing so close, just beyond the window, that the bones beneath his skin, which gave the rugged contours to his face, were very obvious. And the lips, which she looked at next as a diversion from his strong bones, seemed to be sliding towards a smile.

'At least let me drive you,' he said, his eyes—which had drawn a quick glance—repeating the entreaty. 'I mean, it was, as you said, my own quixoticness—quixoticity, I'm not sure of the word—that got you into this. Driving you out and back would be the least I could do to repay you.'

'Repay me for not wanting you there?' Jena asked, but she found her own lips were answering his smile. She just hoped her eyes weren't twinkling!

She had to remind herself of all the reasons she didn't want to be driving back and forth to the lake with Noah, but as he continued to hold the door for her, she couldn't think of one which would sound reasonable said out loud. In the end, she climbed meekly out of the LandCruiser, locked the door and walked across to where he now held the passenger door of the Jeep open for her.

'I'm only doing this because it seems stupid not to travel together,' she told him as he seated himself beside her.

'Heaven forbid I should take it as a craving for my company!' he said. 'I assume that's what you mean?'

Jena shrugged. It came close but more of her reluctance stemmed from her own weakness—her inability to control the way her body reacted to the man.

Right now, the very last thing she needed in her life was a man and the complications a man's intrusion invariably entailed.

Even if she didn't win the job on the challenge, she'd have to find some other new direction, and any new career would need total focus if she was to succeed. She'd tried mixing work and pleasure before, and had lost out on both the relationship and the job she'd wanted. This time she was determined to succeed, to prove, despite what people might think, she was more than just a face with the right look for the moment.

Noah watched the way her brow grew ruffled and recognised it as an outward sign of a mind in turmoil.

'Do you want to talk about it?' he asked, when they were clear of town and he needed less concentration on the task of driving.

She spun to face him, her brow even more furrowed, her eyes puzzled but no less beautiful.

'Talk about what?'

He grinned at the innocence she injected into the question.

'Whatever's troubling you. Sometimes it helps.'

Puzzlement gave way to suspicion.

'Are you in angel-mode again?' she demanded, then she folded her arms across her breasts in a defensive he was beginning to recognise and added, 'And even if you are, this is one thing no angel can work out. It's personal.'

'Love problems?' he persisted, although fairly sure such prying persistence was far from angelic.

'None of your business,' his passenger snapped. Then, as if she didn't want any doubt lingering in his mind, she followed up with an equally snappy, 'No!'

There was a beat of silence, then apparently whatever ire he'd stirred up couldn't be contained for she waded on, 'And why would you ask that question anyway? Are you assuming the only thing that could possibly be on a woman's mind is love? Is such an assumption based on your opinion of the female sex?'

Jena paused for breath, but not for long enough to give him time for rebuttal. 'If you've been spreading it around, some woman probably murdered you. That would fit right in with the angel-in-limbo notion!'

Noah felt his own ire building, and deeply regretted having opened his mouth.

He shouldn't have offered to drive her home—that had been his first mistake.

Or did he have to go back to his rash decision to come to Kareela? Was that where all the trouble had begun?

'Can we forget the angel thing?' he pleaded, as his thoughts worsened, instead of lessening, his confusion. 'I'm real, not much fun, according to you, and possibly quixotic, but flesh and blood nonetheless.'

He heard a murmured comment, but doubted if she'd said what he thought she'd said. Images of flesh of the female variety—softly scented, lightly tanned, yielding—had been making incursions into his mind since he'd first met the woman, but she was a woman who could have had any man she chose, so she was unlikely to be lusting after a confused, usually angry, country doctor like him.

He turned off the highway.

'Have you spoken to the police? Are they happy with the arrangements you've made for Greg and Rose?'

Noah smiled to himself. He must definitely have misheard. Here he was, thinking attraction, and she was thinking of his visitors.

'I spoke to the sergeant as soon as I got to work. I'd phoned him earlier when I found Greg back at the camp site and promised to update him. He'd be remiss if he didn't at least speak to Greg. He'll probably suggest some kind of counselling, but there'll be no criminal charges laid.'

Jena caught the hint of a smile as he considered, then responded to her question. Would it have been a broader smile if he'd known what she'd been thinking? Why she'd had to drag Rose and Greg into the conversation to sidetrack her mind to safer subjects?

Was Noah a modern enough man to accept that women had licentious thoughts about men? Or would he have been shocked to learn of her body's increasingly distracting reaction to his?

She had no idea, but common sense suggested she'd be better off not knowing. Given the problems even a fleeting love affair could generate at the moment, the less she knew of the enigmatic Noah Blacklock the better.

'I'll drop you off then call over to the house to check on them,' he said, his voice startling her out of her thoughts.

'No swim tonight?' Jena queried, as much to make conversation as for any other reason. Dusk was falling fast and she'd already crossed a swim off her immediate 'to do' list.

But Noah surprised her with his reply.

'Maybe later,' he said. 'There'll be an almost full moon tonight so the lake will be well lit. And given it's free of sharks, crocodiles and other predators, we'd be safe enough.'

We'd be safe enough? The words echoed in Jena's head. She had a feeling that swimming in a moonlit lake with this man would be so far removed from safe she shouldn't even contemplate it.

And the dangers she envisaged didn't include sharks or crocodiles.

Although she did feel hot and sticky, and a swim in the moonlight would be magical…

He stopped the car and she hopped out, pleased to have some time to herself so she could make sure she didn't have underwear flung about the place.

But as she walked into the shack and saw the bag Noah had dropped earlier, the enormity of what he'd proposed really struck her. The shack had one room, with a bench in one corner where she'd set up her kitchen. On the back verandah there was a primitive bathroom with a—thankfully—functional lavatory. That's if she tipped a bucket or two of water into the tank each day. There was also a patch of cement under a now-dead shower, where she washed—with another bucket of water.

At least it was private, she reminded herself, looking around the main room once again.

Old wood-framed, canvas camp-stretchers lined the walls, obviously used as somewhere to sit by day and beds at night. She was using one as a cupboard, all her clothing laid in neat piles on it. Warned by Matt, she'd brought a thin rubber mattress to soften the one she slept on—slightly—but Noah wouldn't have such a luxury.

Apart from the beds, there was one chair, rickety, another chair, doubtful, and a table she'd taken all day to scrub before she'd put her box of food on it. She'd spread a piece of bright material she usually wore as a sarong across the rest of it to act as a tablecloth, and that was the extent of her housekeeping.

A rumble of an engine powering through the sand told her Noah had returned, and she moved across to her 'kitchen' and peered into the little gas refrigerator.

She had steaks and more steaks, even a packet of gourmet sausages. The little gas stove had a barbecue plate, and when she'd made her plans, she'd decided grilling meat on it would be the easiest way to prepare a meal.

'Greg and Rose are fine,' her visitor announced, coming into the room and looking around.

The gathering darkness had softened its decrepitude, but Jena still understood that the whistle Noah gave wasn't one of appreciation.

'Shall I light the lamps?' he asked, and Jena chuckled.

'Lamp, singular, and, yes, you can light it. I'm always terrified I'll break the mantle and then have to put on a new one and start all over again.'

He lit the lamp while she started the gas burner under the barbecue plate and dug around in her cool box for the makings of a salad. When she'd tried the refrigerator before leaving home, it had frozen both lettuce and tomatoes, so bringing the cool box had seemed like a good idea, providing she remembered to put a re-frozen ice-brick into it each day.

'I've a folding chair in the back of the Jeep—I'll bring it in,' Noah suggested, then he laughed and added, 'Actually, I've two folding chairs. If you've been sitting on that ancient old thing, you'll end up being grateful I came to stay.'

'Not in this lifetime,' Jena muttered to herself when he was safely out of earshot. Seeing him lighting the lamp and carry it across to the table threw an aura of intimacy around them. Or so her body seemed to think.

Her *mind* definitely didn't want to go there!

'What do you do after dinner? Read? Play patience?'

Noah had returned with the chairs, and though she knew he was only making conversation—which was good as her own supply seemed to have dried up—she didn't want to answer the question with the truth, which was 'go to bed'—which was bad, given the connotation in the words!

'Read a little,' she managed, knowing he'd think there was something wrong if she maintained a stony silence for the entire evening. 'Look at the lake and sky and trees.'

'And I'd thought I was the only one out here, communing with nature.'

His voice had deepened—grown husky—and the tremors along Jena's spine made her so tense she had to shake herself to ease her muscles.

'Steak and salad—perhaps a sausage?'

Noah heard the question, but found it difficult to answer. At some stage, Jena had put on a pair of black-rimmed glasses, presumably so she could read the label on the package she was holding.

And suddenly all he'd ever heard about men not making

passes at girls who wore glasses was proven totally erroneous. Jena Carpenter in glasses was the sexiest thing he'd ever seen.

Even sexier, though he didn't know how it was possible, than Jena Carpenter without them.

'Long-sighted?' he asked, then realised he was back at quarter-witted again. Why else would she be wearing them?

She whipped them off and he was conscious of feeling disappointed he hadn't looked some more while he'd had the chance.

'Very!' she said, her voice as dry as the sand above the high-water mark.

'But you don't need them for driving?'

She shook her head so the blonde hair caught the lamplight and rippled like the reflection of the moon on the lake.

'Only for reading, writing, and computer work.'

As a conversation, it would win prizes for inanity, Noah decided, but he couldn't think of anything better—not even a follow-up.

'Do you eat steak?' she said, saving him the bother, and reminding him she'd already asked the question once.

'Certainly,' he said, then, to make amends, added, 'And salad and sausages.'

He decided he'd give up on conversations and dug around in his hastily packed bag, eventually finding the medical thriller he was currently reading. Discovering occasional medical mistakes in the text hadn't lessened the impact of the tale and he was anxious to get on with it.

Or to immerse himself in something less distracting than thoughts of a bespectacled Jena. Any type of Jena.

He set the book on the table, then realised that as the darkness deepened she'd need the lamp closer to where she was preparing their meal. But there was no way he was going to sit in the corner, even nearer to her. Not even the serial killer within the pages could compete with such proximity.

Jena tried to concentrate on getting a meal together, although tonight the usually simple task was proving difficult. She found Noah's presence in the room distracting in an un-

definable way—almost as if he'd infected the air with something that turned fingers into thumbs and her brain into mush.

With a supreme effort of will she forced herself to concentrate, ignoring the bumping noises he was making, though cu-
rious as to what might be causing them.

She discovered the answer when, after a particularly loud
bump, curiosity won and she turned.

'You've stolen my t-table!' she stuttered.

The accused man stood in the doorway, a dim shape in the
gathering darkness. He chuckled as he crossed the room towards her.

'Simply shifted it outside—onto the front deck. Why eat
indoors when the weather's so great?'

He glanced around her makeshift kitchen.

'I didn't think to bring plates and cutlery. Is there any old
stuff here I can wash and use?'

Jena shook her head, which both answered his question and
woke up a couple of brain cells in the mush.

'I brought enough for two,' she managed, then, as the lamplight revealed a glint of satisfaction in Noah's eyes, she realised her mistake.

'So you were or are expecting Matt to come!' he said, moving closer to peer at the steak she'd just dropped on the hot
plate. 'I like mine rare.'

'You'll get it thrown at you if you don't stop going on about
Matt Ryan!' Jena warned him. 'I've actually enough plates
and so on for four, because rather than pack those things sep-
arately I brought my picnic basket.'

She waved her hand towards the covered basket perched on
the far end of the bench, then angled around her companion
and flipped the steak over.

'You could take the salad out to the table, and you'll find
knives and forks in the basket.'

'Make myself useful, in fact,' Noah said, moving obediently
away.

And get out of my immediate vicinity! Jena added in her
mind.

But she needed him further away. Like on another planet!

Not sitting across a table from her, with lamplight brushing gold across his cheekbones and lighting little fires in his usually cool grey eyes.

They ate in silence, but when the meal was finished the lack of noise seemed to tighten the air between them until the brittle tension forced Jena to break it with speech.

'I visited Carla today.' She spoke brightly, in the hope the false cheer would disguise her uneasiness. 'I didn't meet the others as they were at work, but maybe you can fill me in. How many people are in your programme?'

He looked up, and she thought she saw a fleeting frown tug at his eyebrows, but all he said was, 'It isn't *my* programme. I merely suggested that a town like Kareela, which has a moving population of young people, would be ideal for a halfway house. It seemed to me that the flexibility of this kind of peer group—with people coming and going from it all the time—would make it easier for those on rehab to fit right in.'

'And mixing with the backpackers, hearing about their lives, might give your group an added incentive to stay clean,' Jena said. 'Carla told me that part.'

Noah grinned at her across the table.

'That's actually an added bonus. I knew getting them into a different environment made sense. I mean, to come out of rehab and mix with friends still using didn't seem ideal. But I didn't think of the influence of the travelling young people until much later, when discussions had gone on for so long I wondered if it would ever happen.'

'And you had to come up with a clincher argument?'

He shook his head.

'No! I'd already done that. My aunt had died and left me her house.' He hesitated, looking out over the lake, and Jena wondered if he'd been very close to his aunt and was mourning her loss.

But when he spoke, there was no trace of sadness or nostalgia. More surprise than anything. 'She seemed to think I'd find a worthy use for it—had some idea that because I was a doctor I was also a humanitarian.'

Jena had to smile. Here was another house the man had

given away—but if she wanted to hear the rest of his explanation she'd better not point it out.

'You say that as if the two are mutually exclusive!'

'They often are!' Noah grumbled. 'Why people have this
impression of doctors as the next best thing to saints, I don't
know. A lot of the ones I know are your normal, venial, over-
ambitious human beings clawing their way to the top of whatever particular ladder they've chosen to climb.'

'But not all!' Jena reminded him, thinking of kind and com-
passionate medicos she'd known.

'No, not all,' he said, but his voice lacked conviction.

'Is that why you got off the ladder?' she asked. 'Because
you didn't like what doctors, in your estimation, had become?'

He didn't answer immediately, but looked at the lamp, as
if the bright light might illuminate the question for him.

'I've really no right to criticise anyone else and no, it wasn't
because of what others had become, but for fear of what I
might become myself. That and other things.'

Jena waited for Noah to explain this statement, but he said
nothing more, simply turning his attention from the lamp to
the bush and beyond it to where the lake shone silver in the
moonlight.

'I think I'll take a swim,' he said, then looked doubtfully
at her. 'I don't suppose you want one.'

'Which, translated, means you'd like to go alone,' Jena
sniped. 'Well, tough, because I've had a long day and a swim
is my reward. You don't have exclusive rights on the lake, so
you'll have to put up with me.'

She paused, her mind searching back for an elusive scrap
of memory.

'In fact,' she reminded him, 'not that long ago you invited
me to swim with you. Even guaranteed the water free of things
that bite.'

'I wouldn't be too sure of that!' he said, standing up, gathering the dirty plates and heading back inside the room.

Jena let him go. She'd change into her swimsuit when he

was safely out of the house. And, in the meantime, she had
his irony-laden retort to consider.

The 'I wouldn't be too sure of that' remark!

Seems it matched the thought she'd had earlier!

CHAPTER NINE

EMERGING from the little house some time later, Jena was surprised to find Noah waiting on the steps.

'I thought you'd gone,' she muttered.

'And left you to negotiate this overgrown track on your own? I might not be an angel, but I do have some basic gentlemanly traits. I'll go ahead.'

He also had a torch, which he shone behind him so she could see where she was putting her feet. But no amount of light could ease the tightness in her chest or the awareness of him which sent heat throughout her body.

When they reached the sand she dropped her towel, tucked her hair into a cap and raced towards the water. Cooling off might help. While swimming to the other side and back might tire her sufficiently to enable her to sleep in the same room as him again tonight.

Though she'd probably drown. She could swim well enough to save herself but long-distance swimming wasn't on her CV.

Diving in, she felt the water envelop her, its silky caress soothing frayed nerve endings and cooling the tingling hotness in her blood.

Jena swam about a hundred metres, then rolled over on her back, lazily moving legs and arms to stay afloat while she studied the dark arc of the sky and picked out patterns in the pinpoint brightness of the stars.

'Found the Southern Cross among the stars?' a deep voice asked, but she didn't turn towards Noah. Neither was she startled, as her body had already told her he was near.

'That one's easy,' she said. 'I was actually counting them all tonight. I'd reached one million, four hundred and thirty-five thousand and six, and now you've made me lose my place.'

She flipped over and dived beneath the surface, emerging

closer to the shore and what she hoped was a safe distance away. But he'd followed, porpoising up right beside her, so they stood, in water to their shoulders, less than an arm's length apart.

'The last thing I want in my life is a romantic entanglement!' he said bluntly, and Jena, pleased to have the silent menace out in the open, smiled.

'Entanglement doesn't begin to describe how devastating a love affair would be for me right now!' she told him. 'It would ruin everything!'

There, it was said—though saying it didn't stop her moving towards him when he touched her shoulder, didn't stop her body pressing against his, or her lips answering some silent demand for kisses.

Eventually they had to stop for breath.

'If this was real, I'd rather be kissing you on dry land so I could see your hair all around your shoulders. So I could touch it and feel it and run my fingers through it. It's fascinated me, your hair!'

Jena looked into his face, shadowy but intent.

'If this was real, I'd probably take off the cap, but without power for a hair-dryer, I'd still be wet-haired in the morning. So, as it isn't real, and it's not something serious, you'll have to make do with the cap.'

She leaned into a second kiss, feeling the smoothness of his lips, thrilling to the explorations of his tongue, wondering why kissing one man should be so exciting when recent kisses she'd experienced had had all the appeal of kissing a dead fish.

'Are you concentrating?' he demanded, lifting his head to look into her eyes. She had to laugh.

'Not really,' she told him. 'I mean, it's not serious—not something we both want. More like an experiment, isn't it? But it's nice. Better by far than kissing a dead fish!'

His turn to laugh. In fact, he laughed so hard he pulled away, leaving a sense of desolation in Jena's skin.

'Well, I'm glad I beat the fish!' he said, reaching out to take her hand and towing her towards the shore.

It was nice, she decided, being able to laugh with him.

'We could be friends.' She spoke aloud because the revelation was overwhelming.

'Do you think so?' he said, with the same cynicism she'd heard in his voice when he'd spoken of doctors' ambition.

'There's no reason why not!' she said stoutly. 'After all, we'll be working together for the next few weeks and living together for a few days. Wouldn't it be easier if we were friends instead of arguing all the time?'

'Friends don't kiss the way we just did,' he reminded her, turning towards her now they'd reached water's edge. 'Like this, remember?'

He slipped the cap off her head then tangled his fingers in her hair to draw her head towards him.

With a soft sigh of something she didn't want to think about, she kissed him back, revelling in the firmness of his body against her curves, the cool dampness of his skin against her heat.

'We won't keep kissing,' she told him, when once again they paused to regain control of their breathing and suck in some much-needed air. 'I mean, we don't have to, do we? Neither of us wants a relationship right now, so probably it's best if we don't.'

She felt his hand on her hair again, only gently this time, smoothing through the tangles.

'Definitely best if we don't,' he agreed, but for the first time since she'd met him she heard an echo of uncertainty in his voice.

Definitely best if we don't, she repeated to herself as that faint echo weakened her resolve. She stepped away, found her towel and rubbed it hard across her body.

'Why are you so against romantic entanglements?' she asked, wanting to know but also wanting to start a conversation, any conversation, to bring some sanity back into her life. 'A bad experience? A life plan it would wreck?'

She heard Noah's feet crunch in the sand but he didn't stop beside her although his footsteps slowed.

'Are you asking out of idle curiosity or do you really want to know?'

Jena thought about it for a moment.

'I was making conversation when I asked, but I would like to know. I mean, if we're going to be friends, it's the kind of thing we could talk about.'

'Fair enough!' he said, but he told her nothing, merely shining the torch behind him as he picked his way back up the track. She followed, wondering if he intended talking later. Wondering what she'd got herself into, and how she'd reply if he happened to ask her the same thing.

Noah let his feet find their own way along the path. His brain was too bemused to be giving orders.

Why the hell, when a woman had stated very bluntly the last thing on earth she wanted was a love affair, had he gone ahead and kissed her?

And why, after she'd compared him, favourably as it happened, to a dead fish, had he done it again?

Now she was wanting to talk about things—didn't all women?

As for being friends…

He reached the bottom of the steps.

'I'll make coffee,' he told her, then remembered that the food supplies he'd taken from his place were still in the back of the Jeep.

'When I've got the rest of my stuff out,' he added, and walked around the little building instead of entering it.

He knew she'd followed him because his body had become attuned to her presence. Even at the hospital he could make a good guess as to where she was from some kind of supersensitivity meter he'd recently developed in his skin.

'I'll help you carry things,' she said, as if he'd asked why.

He didn't argue. Though he'd only known her for two days, he'd learnt the futility of *that* exercise!

'You can take the box, I'll take the fridge,' he said, when he'd opened the rear of the Jeep and an interior light came on to reveal his hastily packed stores. 'The McDonalds had their own stuff and insisted they didn't want any of mine,' he added, as she leaned past him, inadvertently giving him a tantalising glimpse of the deep shadow between her full breasts.

Friends?

But she was right, they could hardly remain at war with each other when they had to share such cramped quarters by night and see each other at work every day.

He'd had women friends before, he reminded himself as she walked away, the moonlight revealing the rhythm of her gliding elegance, not in the least marred by the burden she was carrying.

Not women friends he'd kept wanting to kiss!

He hefted the straps of his swag across one shoulder, then picked up the small refrigerator and stalked towards the house. All he had to do was stop kissing her, he told himself. He didn't have to promise to be friends, or even try very hard to achieve that. He just had to stop the kissing.

He yelled this last order in his head, but doubted if the added intensity would make any difference. She was so entirely kissable.

And kissing someone didn't necessarily lead to complications like relationships.

Did it?

He carried his burdens up the steps, across the verandah and into the house, dropping the swag by one of the camp stretchers and continuing on to the kitchen corner with the fridge. The box Jena had carried was sitting on the bench, but there was no sign of his hostess.

Probably in the bathroom! He breathed easier as the thought of Jena changing into night attire in front of him had been only one of the tormenting images flashing through his head. He filled the kettle from one of the drums of water she had stacked beneath the bench and made a mental note to take the empty one to town the following day and refill it.

Surely he could do those little things to make life easier for her without treading on her independent toes.

He found matches and lit the gas, thinking now of the ten pink toes he'd seen as she'd floated in the moonlight. Wondering how they'd taste.

Enough! Noah told his wayward mind, but at that stage his sensory perception told him she was back and he glanced towards the door and decided it would have been easier to watch her change her clothes than see her like this, in a long white gown of material so fine that, with the moon behind her, it hid none of the contours of her body.

Though he'd seen quite a bit of them already. The swimsuit had clung so lovingly she might as well have been naked.

But this garment was torment, plain and simple. It suggested, it hinted and it teased.

'What?' she demanded, obviously picking up on his reaction for she glanced down at herself. 'It covers me from neck to well below the knee, it's cotton so it doesn't cling. What's to look at?'

'It's…' he began, then had to stop and find some moisture for his mouth so he could start again. 'N-nothing, n-nothing at all!' he stammered, deciding that the old saying about discretion being the better part of valour might hold true right now. 'You came in so quietly I was surprised.'

'Thought I was a ghost, did you?' Jena joked, coming closer and fortunately moving into the shadows so he could no longer see right through the material.

As long as she didn't stand between him and the lamp. He'd have to be aware of the danger. Be careful. He couldn't afford too many glimpses of filmily draped contours if he wanted to avoid kissing her again.

'So, are you going to answer my question?' she demanded as he prepared her coffee, black and unsweetened as he'd watched her drink it the previous day. He set it on the bench, then suggested they sit outside and led the way so he didn't have to watch her body move as he followed her.

'Or continue to avoid it?' she persisted.

'You're like one of those sticky flies. No matter how many times you brush it away, it always seems to come back.'

Jena chuckled softly.

'I guess I can't complain about animal—or insect—comparisons, having already mentioned dead fish!'

'Definitely not,' he said, 'though I'm intrigued to know

more about the fish. Presumably you must have found something you liked about the man to have kissed him.'

'Oh, he wasn't any man in particular, just a generalisation about the effect of some kisses.'

'On which subject you're, no doubt, an expert!' Noah said, and heard a hint of his gut-tightening reaction in the terseness of the words.

'Definitely!' she said, as cheerfully as if kissing were an everyday occurrence for the entire world. 'I've had the wet-fish ones, the tight-lipped pressure-mashers that leave the inner lining of your lips in tatters, the tongue thrust down to tangle in your tonsils type. In fact, I've often wondered why more research hasn't been done. You know how someone's always telling you something about yourself from the way you sit, or hold your hands, or the colours you wear? What about kiss analysis?'

Noah found himself wanting to ask if he was a lip-masher or a tonsil-tangler but knew he mightn't like the answer so he refrained. But the talk of kissing was getting to him—and the way she spoke, so offhand about her experience, made things even worse.

'It might be handy, then, this forced proximity,' he said, hoping he sounded less nervous about this suggestion than he felt. 'Perhaps, as you're obviously an expert on the subject, you can give me some tips on what women like in the way of kisses. Just as a friend, of course.'

The silence that greeted this suggestion seemed to thunder in his ears, though he wasn't so confused that he didn't know silence couldn't possibly be heard!

He sneaked a look across the table to see if he could guess at her reaction, but her chair was drawn back into the dark shadow of the eaves and all he could discern was the pale oval of her face and the shimmering beauty of the cascading hair.

She reached out to pick up her coffee, took a sip, then cradled the mug in her hands.

'I don't know!' she finally replied. 'As a teacher I'd probably be a dunce, and most of what I know is hearsay, anyway.

I imagine really good kisses have to start deep in the soul and grow with feelings, not just mechanical skill.'

'But surely there has to be some mechanics involved,' Noah protested, as the hope of kissing her again in the immediate future was dashed to the ground. 'We could practise that part.'

'We already did,' she reminded him. 'And got it right. Which should be enough of a warning for anyone who doesn't want to get involved to back right off.'

She stood up, still cradling the coffee mug as if she needed to draw warmth from its heat.

'I think I'll take this to bed,' she said. 'I've a small battery lamp I read by, so you can have the gas light.'

He watched her disappear into the interior, the lamp, still on the kitchen bench, throwing shadows across the room as she moved about. Bedclothes rustled, old canvas creaked, and he knew she was settling onto the uncomfortable camp stretcher.

By the time he followed her into the room she had a small lamp lit and was sitting up in bed, long slim fingers moving through her hair as she plaited the silky tresses into a loose braid.

'Pity this castle hasn't a tower,' he murmured. 'We could have played Rapunzel and the Prince.'

'My hair isn't long enough for Rapunzel,' she told him, snuffing out his little fantasy. 'And while I've not quite given up on the quixotic angel theory, I'm pretty sure you're no prince.'

He had to laugh, then he carried his bag over closer to the lamp, found what he'd need for his pre-bed ablutions and left the room, determined to pull himself together before he re-entered it. The way things were going at the moment, with his imagination overheated to boiling point, he'd never get to sleep.

Jena woke to daylight, and an awareness she wasn't alone. It didn't take long for all the pieces to click into place and she raised her head cautiously from her pillow and looked across the room.

Noah slept, but quietly, not even the sound of his breathing carrying across the space.

She studied him, or what she could see of him. His dark hair was rumpled, his strong features relaxed, but still well defined by a bone structure which would withstand the ravages of time and keep him handsome well into old age.

Shoulders, broad and strong—she'd noticed them the first day when he'd changed her tyre. Swimmer's shoulders. She'd guessed from the ease with which he'd cut through the water that he'd probably trained at some time.

He lay on his side so she could see one arm bent forward, a mist of silky dark hair on his forearm lying flat against his skin.

All in all, an extremely good-looking man, but with intelligence as well. So why had he forsaken a good position in the city? And what had happened to make him so adamant he didn't want a relationship?

He opened his eyes as if her scrutiny had wakened him, and looked directly at her, neither blinking nor, apparently, confused.

'You tell me first,' he said, and she knew exactly what he was talking about. 'Then I'll tell you.'

It was a dare and she guessed he thought she'd back away. Instead, she sat up and swung her legs out of bed.

'My reason's easy. I've a new challenge ahead of me—well, I hope I have, this job should prove it—one that will take me away for months at a time. I believe all relationships, especially at the beginning, need a lot of nurturing. They're like little seedlings which require more attention than established plants. Being away for long periods of time puts them at risk. That's why, right now, I don't need any complications in my life, particularly personal ones.'

'You don't have a very high opinion of men, do you?' he murmured, mirroring her movements by sitting up and swinging his own legs out of bed. 'Dead fish, mouth-mashers and now lumped together as "complications". I find it hard to believe so much cynicism could be contained in such a beautiful package.'

Jena grinned at him as she stood up and crossed to the door to look out at the lake in the early morning light.

'It's the beautiful packaging, if you care to call it that—which I don't—that's one of the causes of the problem.' She threw the words over her shoulder as she stretched the kinks out of her spine. 'A lot of people don't bother looking beyond the ribbons and wrapping.'

'When you're standing in the doorway, I can see way past the wrapping,' Noah growled, and Jena felt a rush of heat as she realised exactly what he meant.

She turned and fled back to the bed, grabbed a sheet and wrapped it around her body, then hurried out the back door to the bathroom where a good splash of cold water from the drum she kept out there cooled her flushed face and restored a little of her equilibrium.

'Still friends?' he asked, when she came tentatively back inside.

'You might have told me you could see right through my nightdress,' she complained.

His answering smile was totally unrepentant.

'Oh, but I did!' he reminded her, and Jena had to content herself with a growly, mumbled threat that made her sound like a school kid.

Crossing to the bed, she pulled the elastic band off her plait and unwound the braid, then picked up her brush and began her usual morning task of dragging out all the tangles.

Noah carried his breakfast of cereal and fruit onto the verandah. At least out there he wouldn't have to watch the curiously intimate routine of hair-brushing. And if images of himself wielding the brush, pulling the bristles through the shining fall, were running riot in his head, they might be more easily controlled when he wasn't watching her.

By the time Jena joined him, dressed for work, but with her hair still loose, he'd regained enough equilibrium to remember her opening statement of the morning.

'What kind of a challenge would be ruined by a man?'

She looked surprised, then seemed to realise what he was referring to.

'By *any* complication, not necessarily a man!' she told him, setting down a breakfast similar to his own. 'And I can't tell you because it's all still hush-hush. New television projects are always wrapped in cloaks of secrecy for fear some other channel will pinch the idea first.'

He suspected she was laughing inwardly at this concept, so pursued his questioning.

'And this kind of paranoia doesn't put you off?'

She laughed out loud now, the delightful notes ringing out, frightening a small blue tit which had been perched in a banksia just beyond the verandah.

'It's nothing to the paranoia among designers. Most of them would like to cut the tongues from all models so the secrets of their new season's collections remain safe until the showing.' She paused to spoon cereal into her delectable mouth. 'In fact, I was so inured to it I took it as normal when I entered the world of television.'

'Hmm,' Noah murmured. Hardly the most intelligent of responses but all he could manage after watching the way the tip of her pink tongue, fortunately not removed for secrecy, had emerged to swipe a tiny crumb of wheat flake from her lower lip.

'Now it's your turn,' she said, as cheerful as the sunshine reflecting brightly off the lake.

'Maybe later,' he said, when he realised explaining would mean telling her about Lucy, and right now he didn't want to bring another woman into the conversation.

Though he could tell her about Amy—do it that way.

He was still considering this when an unfamiliar noise broke the silence.

'Damn! My phone. That'll be Matt. I'm supposed to phone him every morning to assure him I've made it safely through another night, and I always forget!'

Jena left the table, her long legs carrying her effortlessly away from Noah towards another man—even if he *was* only on the phone.

Brightness faded from the day and the sense of well-being that had settled, with breakfast, in his body disappeared, to be replaced by a scrungy feeling he couldn't—or didn't want to—identify.

Of course there must be something going on between her and Matt. Maybe he was the project she was keeping so secret. Had she targeted the womanising television star and executive as husband material?

Noah felt regret sidle into his heart and had to remind himself it was none of his business. In fact, given the kissability of the woman and his own determination to stay free of attachments for a while, it was probably a very good thing if Matt *was* the project.

Perhaps he could help her reach her goal.

Noah grinned to himself.

Knowing Matt's legendary determination to not get married, helping Jena catch him might be fun—as well as sweet revenge for Bridget Somerton.

And for all those years of having him held up as the paragon of all virtues.

'You're looking very cheerful for someone who's going to be late for work if he doesn't get dressed within the next two minutes.'

The remark made him forget the puzzle of why the anticipated revenge wasn't tasting as sweet as he'd expected, and he clambered hurriedly to his feet, mumbled something about being right back and disappeared into the house.

Of course, his clothes were still in a suit bag in the car, so he had to dash out there, then have a quick shave in cold water, splash himself more or less clean, and dress so hurriedly his clothes kept sticking to his barely dry body.

'I'm going to put in a hand-held shower of some kind,' he growled when he found Jena waiting with an exaggerated air of impatience by the Jeep.

'That'd be good,' she agreed. 'Will you organise a new tank and speak to God about some rain to fill it, or do some showers come with their own water supply?'

'OK, I know it won't be easy!' he told her, climbing into the car and slamming the door.

'And it will be cold unless you also work out heating,' she

reminded him, then her lips tilted into a smile so teasingly delightful he forgot how to breathe. 'Don't tell me you're regretting the generous but erratic impulse that made you lend your place to Greg and Rose?'

The answer should have been a shouted 'yes' because, if nothing more, staying in his own place would have meant less contact with this beautiful witch!

'No!' he said, when the ability to form words finally returned. Then, in case she didn't get the message, he repeated it more firmly.

'No!'

CHAPTER TEN

THE drive to the highway began in silence, but Jena couldn't let it hang between them.

'It's your turn,' she reminded Noah. 'I told you, now you tell me.'

He glanced her way and grinned.

'And if I said, "Jena, don't go on and on", would you stop?'

She had to smile—perhaps there was a fun gene buried somewhere in his psyche.

'No!' she told him. 'Fair's fair.'

His sigh was strong enough to bounce off the windscreen but he didn't speak.

'Who did you buy the house for?'

He started as if she'd bitten him.

'What house? What do you mean, who did I buy it for?'

'You know what house—the one where Carla and co. are temporarily living. It's not the kind of house a man intending to live alone would buy for himself, so there's a woman in the story somewhere.'

Another sigh riffled through the air between them.

'Sticky flies have nothing on you,' he muttered. 'I have a friend—a close friend—actually, we've had something going for a few years now—more than a few...'

'Boy! That sounds like a great relationship!' Jena snorted. 'Something going? More than a few years? Is this a love affair or an occasionally convenient bit of sex? How does she describe it? Does she use the same words or might she use the dreaded "love" word?'

'It's really none of your business, but you asked. If you don't like the answer, that's too bad!'

His scowl had returned and tension whitened his knuckles on the steering wheel.

'OK, I'll accept that whatever it was between you, it suited both of you—or you, anyway. But if it was OK, why the avoidance now? Why the remarks about no relationships this century?'

Noah laughed instead of sighing this time.

'You do go on and on, don't you? Actually, I guess your reaction irritated me because it put into words what Lucy tried to tell me—about something missing in our relationship. I took it she wanted marriage, commitment, a mapped-out future—together. So I bought the house up here, did the whole proposal thing—bended knee, ring, the lot—and she roared with laughter.'

And though he'd laughed before he'd spoken, there was no mirth in the words of explanation. Jena felt her heart grow heavy with sympathy for him.

'What *did* she want?' she asked, not needing to know any more but feeling, now he'd started talking, it might help him to finish.

He shrugged.

'None of the things I wanted, apparently. I'd often talked about shifting to a large country town eventually, because I believe it's a better environment for bringing up children. She'd never said it wouldn't suit her, never even hinted at it.'

'And?'

'Apparently she'd thought I wasn't serious—that it was all just hot air. She's ambitious—another doctor—and she'd assumed I was just as keen to climb the ladder. In fact, she'd assumed that after my years in Emergency I'd specialise in critical care. When I told her I'd given notice to the hospital and had been appointed at Kareela, she told me I must be mad.'

They were on the highway now, caught in the slow lane behind a school bus.

'You resigned, got a new job and bought a house, all without telling the woman to whom you were about to propose?' Jena couldn't hide her incredulity. 'I can understand the limpness of the "something going" phrase now. For two people who'd presumably had a lengthy relationship, you didn't know each other too well. How could you both be so totally wrong about each other?'

'I thought I knew her,' he muttered defensively, then he swung out from behind the bus and accelerated past it.

'She probably thought she knew you, until you informed her you were both off to the country! What on earth did she say? How did it turn out?'

Noah knew he couldn't sigh again. He glanced towards his passenger. If he refused to answer, would she persist?

Of course she would. She was a woman.

A particularly persistent one!

'She told me I was mad, then tried to talk me out of it and finally admitted the relationship had grown very stale anyway, so much so she'd had the odd affair with colleagues, and finished by agreeing it would be a good idea if I *did* come up here. I could get the country thing out of my system and if we spent the year apart, saw other people, maybe we could recapture whatever had drawn us together.'

'Which was probably sex,' Jena told him bluntly, then she turned towards him, shaking her head and frowning. 'And you went along with this? What are you going to do when the year's up? Go meekly back to the city? And if she hasn't found anyone she likes better, continue with a relationship that wasn't offering enough for you to understand each other?'

'What human being ever understands another?' he growled, because the way Jena made it sound, the whole thing was pathetic. And his behaviour, seen through another's eyes, must be even more pitiable. He should have finished with Lucy right then and there, rather than going along with her suggestion that something special might rise again from the ashes of their relationship.

He wasn't a psychologist but he guessed that not finalising things—not ending the relationship cleanly—made the anger he felt over her betrayal worse. What he'd told himself was mature behaviour might simply be avoidance!

'Most people can make a bit of an effort to understand each other!' Jena pointed out. 'And you must have some empathy for your fellow man to be giving away houses the way you do.'

'I don't give away houses!'

He swung the car off the highway and slowed down as they entered town. Talking about Lucy had reignited all the tension he'd thought he could leave behind him, so his stomach felt knotted and a tightness in his temples suggested a headache wasn't too far away.

Then Jena Carpenter patted him on the knee.

His involuntary reaction caused him to start, but the comfort of the casual touch eased some of the knots. Until she said, 'Well, I think it's a very nice house, and your Lucy would have been lucky to get it! Was it decorated when you bought it or did you do the colours yourself?'

He glanced towards her, wondering if she could be psychic.

'I had a decorator do the colours,' he said, the words bringing back the first of his post-Lucy disasters.

Sally had been recommended by a friend, and while she'd been consulting with him over what Lucy might want she'd been friendly but nothing more. Then he'd made the mistake of telling her about Lucy's reaction to the beautiful home she'd created, and Sally's offer to comfort him after his split with Lucy had led to a situation which should have taught him the lesson he'd finally learnt with Linda. To keep his professional and personal lives separate!

And to avoid all relationships, no matter how casual, until he knew for certain it was what he wanted.

Which meant he had to stop kissing Jena!

Because even if she turned out to be exactly what he wanted, she'd made it abundantly clear that she wanted this hush-hush job she was after far more than she wanted a man in her life.

Embarrassed by the impulse that had made her touch him, and the silence that had followed his last reply, Jena turned her attention to Carla's problems.

'By the way, Carla mentioned a library. Do you know where it is?'

He didn't seem to find her question at all unusual, for he

merely nodded and said, 'I'll drive you past on the way to the hospital.'

Aware, from the distracted way he spoke, that he was thinking of something else, hopefully not her hand patting his knee, she took the opportunity to study him. In profile, his face had too many angles to be conventionally handsome, but the long nose, slightly bumped in the middle, and high forehead balanced out the determined thrust of his chin.

Was it always so determined? Or so jutted?

She didn't think so, and wondered what was occupying his mind.

Not what was occupying hers, that was for sure. One glimpse of those lips and back came the memories of how they'd felt when he'd kissed her. Spine-tingling, that's how it had been—and even now, remembering, faint reverberations trickled down her backbone.

'What are your plans for the day? Apart from following me around?' He asked the questions as he took the turn before the one they usually used.

A quick analysis of his voice suggested he was asking out of politeness and wasn't particularly interested in her reply.

'I might give you a miss,' she told him—serve him right for assuming! 'I want to spend time with the nursing staff, following them through their routines. Then the ancillary staff—there's plenty to do.'

'Yes?' Noah asked, and Jena had to smile at his patent disbelief.

'Give us a chance!' she suggested. 'Relax a little and you might find you actually enjoy having the buzz in the air when a production's in progress.'

He turned towards her as if the suggestion he relax—or perhaps it was the idea of enjoyment—was too bizarre to contemplate.

'Fun, remember?'

'That's the library,' he said, ignoring Jena's dig and waving one long-fingered hand towards a small brick building. 'I think it's open every day, but one of the women in the office could tell you for sure. Did you want to find something special?'

'Statues!' she told him, then took pity on his bewilderment and explained.

'I suppose you're aware you're making more work for yourself,' he said. 'All for nothing when you consider the reason the council has a parade in Kareela. I bet it's to get people into the main street, near the shops, where doubtless they'll spend money. I think Christmas is grossly over-commercialised as it is.'

Jena let him grumble, though her mind was gnawing at the problem of the strange personality of the man.

He was generous, evidenced by this giving away of houses to all and sundry, yet, as she'd pointed out to him already, he seemed to get no pleasure from the act of giving. In fact, in spite of a few glimpses she'd had of a softer Noah Blacklock, he was the most uptight man she'd ever met.

Was the generosity a penance of some kind?

Then there was the financial inducement from the television company, yet there was no way she could see him as a greedy man—

They were turning into the big car park at the rear of the hospital, but Jena asked the question anyway.

'The extra money offered by the film company,' she began. 'Did you want it for the drug rehabilitation project? Does it cost money? I know the young people are living in your house at present, but didn't you say there was another house? Will they have to rent? Won't they earn money with their fruit-picking? Shouldn't they be aiming towards financial independence as well as being drug-free?'

He steered the Jeep neatly into a parking space and turned off the engine. Half smiled as he turned towards her.

'So many questions and so little time,' he said, nodding towards where the crew were gathered near the back door, apparently waiting for her. 'Did you save them up for the last minute or have they just occurred to you?'

But Jena didn't answer, too busy thinking of the consequences of the crew seeing her getting out of Noah Blacklock's vehicle.

Damn!

They wouldn't necessarily tell Matt because she doubted whether he had much to do with underlings this far down the chain of command, but they'd certainly think the worst and give her some grief.

'Damn!'

She said it out loud this time, then realised Noah had been talking to her and she'd ignored him.

'I'm sorry, can we talk about it tonight? Right now, I'd better find work for this lot to be doing to keep their smutty minds off what they'll be thinking about you and me. I thought by now they'd have been upstairs, hammering the walls of your mock office.'

She pushed open the car door and was surprised when Noah appeared to hold it for her. For a big man, he could move with remarkable speed.

'I'll see you some time during the day?' he asked.

She looked into his eyes and saw a gleam that made answering impossible.

Well, nearly impossible.

'I suppose so,' she managed to croak, then the gleam turned mischievous and before she could move away he leaned forward and kissed her on the lips.

'If they're going to talk anyway, we might as well give them some ammunition.'

The murmured words felt warm against her skin, and a kind of glow started in her blood.

'Oh, hell!' she muttered, because she couldn't think of anything else to say, then she ducked past him and hurried towards the winking, nudging, chiacking members of the crew.

Noah entered the building through Outpatients, glad it was the film crew, not hospital staff members, who'd seen them arrive together. Though would the staff have cared? He'd been here five months and although he knew everyone, and all of them were very polite, he couldn't say he'd made any friends.

Perhaps Rhoda...

She appeared on cue, meeting up with him in the hall outside the men's ward.

'Linda Carthew's looking for you. She's in the foyer,' the

nursing sister said. 'I'd say she wants to talk to you about the parade. Says she meant to bring it up at yesterday's meeting but you sidetracked her with something else.'

Rhoda paused and Noah realised there was worse to come.

'Apparently the board wants the hospital to participate and all staff members to be involved.'

Noah gaped at her.

'Participate how?' he demanded, and Rhoda chuckled.

'I'm sure she'll tell you,' she said, then she ducked away, still laughing to herself.

'We thought a float. You could do it like a hospital ward but make it fun,' Linda told him. 'I've already discussed it with Jeff and he thinks it's a great idea.'

Noah clamped his teeth together and again resisted the temptation to roll his eyes. He could just imagine it! People in white coats pretending to be doctors, wearing glasses with big noses and bushy eyebrows attached, chasing patients with huge hypodermic needles while nurses in short uniforms bent over beds and revealed plenty of leg.

'I don't know that I'll have time to be involved,' he said, then he remembered Jena telling him of Carla's plan to do something and seized on it as an excuse. 'I've promised I'd help the young people at my house put something together. They want to give something back to the town.'

Linda's polite smile faded and a spark of anger flickered in her eyes.

'Surely the hospital should have first call on your availability, Noah.' She spoke calmly but he could hear the menace underneath.

'During working hours, of course,' he agreed, speaking carefully to avoid exacerbating the problems between them. 'But this will be an after-hours project, and the parade is on a Saturday. I'll probably be on call, but not on duty, Linda.'

She spun around and strode away, every step she took indicating just how angry she was.

'She really does hate you, doesn't she?'

Jena had appeared behind him, and Noah wondered if her arrival had been an added aggravation for Linda.

'It could be partly my fault,' he said, speaking his thoughts aloud because he found the level of Linda's anger disturbing. 'When I first arrived in town, she invited me to dinner, and I assumed she was doing it on behalf of the board. In return, I took her to dinner. There's a wonderful restaurant out by the river and we went there. Then the local theatre group was putting on a play and she had tickets—'

'You went out with her and then you dumped her.' Jena said, correctly interpreting Linda's view of the events. 'And you say it's only *partly* your fault!'

'I didn't dump her!' Noah protested. 'Dumping someone—and that's an awful word, by the way—assumes there was a relationship in the first place, which there wasn't. In fact, just as soon as I realised what was happening, I told her I wasn't interested in a relationship right then.'

Jena smiled at him.

'Well, at least you learnt from the experience. You made sure I had that information almost as soon as we met—or, at least, as soon as we started living together! Though I thought that's what your year apart from Lucy was all about—seeing other people, having other relationships!'

She gave him a saucy smile and went lightly up the steps, her long legs flashing as she took them in her usual energetic fashion, two at a time.

She'd disappeared around the corner before he realised he hadn't told her he'd volunteered himself to help his 'druggies', as the town called them, with their parade preparations.

Not for any worthy reason, he reminded himself, though Jena wasn't to know it.

Noah poked his head into the office to check there was nothing urgent needing his attention and, once reassured, began his ward round. Mrs Burns's throat infection was finally responding to the drugs—or so he assumed when his patient informed him she was feeling a lot better.

He took another swab to be sure and moved on. Mrs Nevins, not technically his patient but still his responsibility while in hospital, was reacting well to the new blood-pressure medication her GP was trying, and young Toby had stabilised and now wanted to finish the chess game they'd been playing in snatched moments and then go home.

All the other patients were doing well, and the realisation that they could possibly be doing equally well without him made him consider Jeff Finch's contention that Kareela hospital didn't need a full-time medico.

The wail of a siren, growing louder and seemingly more urgent as the vehicle drew near, put a stop to such negative thoughts. He walked through to the emergency room, met Marion and a wardsman and all three of them walked out to meet the ambulance.

'Pregnant woman gone into premature labour,' the ambulance driver told them as he got out of the vehicle and came around to the back door.

His coworker was crouched in the back, his head bent over the woman as he reassured her.

'Her name's Minnie Cooke, and all she seems to know is that the baby isn't due until February. She kept telling us it couldn't come because destiny had decreed she have an Aquarian.'

The man looked as puzzled as Noah felt as he tried to make sense of this information, but the stretcher had been rolled from the ambulance by now, so he forgot about destiny to concentrate on the here and now.

'We put her on a drip and attached an external electronic foetal monitor,' the second attendant told Noah, who was introducing himself to the young woman.

She grasped his hand and held on tightly.

'Don't let me lose the baby,' she begged, her dark eyes so full of pain Noah felt his heart contract. He walked beside her as she was wheeled into the emergency room. As if by osmosis, Jena had appeared, and was again doing her unobtrusive thing in the background.

'We'll do whatever we can,' he promised Minnie. 'But you'll have to help me. Do you know how many weeks pregnant you are, or when the baby's due? And who's your usual doctor?'

The young woman sighed.

'I don't know the weeks and we don't have a doctor, but the baby is due in early February.'

Quick mental arithmetic suggested the labour was danger-ously early. A second assessment of his patient explained the 'don't have a doctor' statement. The wild, dishevelled hair and colourful sari-style attire suggested she was part of a small self-sufficient community of young people who lived in the hills not far from the town. Hippie-folk, the town called them, using an expression left over from the sixties.

As he read the information on the ambulance's treatment sheet—strong uterine contractions lasting forty seconds, oc-curring every ten minutes though the interval was reducing, but the foetal heartbeat was good—he worked out the likely background. Then he turned his attention back to the patient.

'Did you have any inkling this might happen? Any recent discomfort, loss of fluid, backache, cramps, other pain?'

'I've been tireder than I was and I've been feeling uncom-fortable, kind of bloated, but didn't think anything of it until the pains started in the night.'

Which meant they'd been going for some time before she'd reached out for help, Noah realised.

'Here's what we're going to do,' he told her. 'For a start, we'll examine you and make sure it is pre-term labour, then we'll try to stop it with fluids and drugs.'

He saw her flinch from the word 'drugs' but she didn't argue.

'And at the same time, in case we can't stop it, we'll give you a steroid treatment which will help the baby's lungs and possibly prevent some of the complications of prematurity.'

'I don't want to have the baby now!'

'We don't want you to either,' Noah assured her, then he nodded to Marion to take over as comforter while he began his examination.

The cervix was dilated but the membranes were intact—one big bonus.

'We'll do an ultrasound, make sure there's plenty of fluid around the baby, check on its gestational age and how it's lying,' Noah told Minnie, but kept back the information that the ultrasound would also show up any congenital abnormality which might have brought on the premature labour.

No need for her to worry about that yet.

'Perhaps we should send her straight to the city,' Marion suggested. 'The helicopter could be here in half an hour and have her in Brisbane in less than two hours.'

Noah, who'd been wondering the same thing himself, hesitated.

'Let's see if we can stabilise her first. After all, it would be very awkward delivering on the helicopter, and if you consider fifty per cent of preterm labour resolves itself, it seems a pity to send her even further away from home. Fluid resuscitation will often stave it off as well.'

He paused, but sensed Marion still had doubts.

'We've a Humidicrib if she did deliver. Should that happen, then both mother and child can be whisked away to the city.'

Where an overworked and overtired young intern would probably be the first person to see them! Noah was confident he could do better himself, but didn't like to say so.

Treatment with magnesium sulphate had a good degree of safety, though at its higher levels it could cause headaches and possible respiratory depression.

The ultrasound showed a small foetus, but no lack or excess of fluid. No other abnormalities were obvious and Noah was convinced they could safely keep Minnie in Kareela a little longer.

'I'm going to start you on magnesium sulphate, which works to stop whatever is telling your body it's ready to deliver,' he told Minnie. In fairness to her, he added, 'This is probably the first line of treatment you'd get anywhere. We'll keep the foetal heart monitor on you so we can monitor the baby's heart, and I'll have a nurse with you at all times in case the labour increases.'

The anxiety in her eyes seemed to lessen, but he had to add the option.

'Or, if you'd prefer, we could transfer you by helicopter to Brisbane where you'd have specialist obstetricians and paediatricians available should you need them.'

'I don't want to go to Brisbane,' she murmured, confirming Noah's guess. 'Not unless I really have to.'

Marion nodded at Noah as if to say, You're right, and he went ahead, working out dosages while Marion and a young aide took Minnie through to one of the rooms used as maternity suites.

As the gurney was wheeled away, Jena fell in behind the staff, while he took the swabs and urine through to the lab. Kits enabled most country doctors to do basic tests and he prepared slides for cultures and checked on the obvious. Other samples would still go to the pathology laboratory in the city to confirm what he'd found—or not found—and in case their more sophisticated tests revealed abnormalities.

All he wanted was confirmation that it was safe to start drug treatment.

He knew it was Jena who'd entered the room, although, bent over the microscope, he hadn't seen her enter.

'Marion felt I should be watching whatever you'd doing now,' she said, her faintly scented presence dominating the room.

'Running a few tests—not terribly photogenic or exciting stuff.'

He inched along the bench, taking out the colour codes to check against the treated specimen—and hoping to get further away from her. But she followed, peering through the eyepiece of the microscope he'd just abandoned.

'In fact, none of it's exciting, as I told the first person who came. You want action, you need a city hospital.'

She lifted her head to look at him while he continued to satisfy himself there wasn't any reason he couldn't give Minnie magnesium sulphate.

'It isn't action they want but reality,' Jena explained. 'The whole point of the series is to show the contrast between the television series and the real thing. This is only one segment— they're doing fire stations, emergency rescue services, a city hospital emergency room, the water police and a metropolitan police station, because all of these have had fictional TV series made about them. Whatever the crew film here will be edited and segments of the real thing will be contrasted against a similar segment from a fictional show.'

'Sounds to me a comparison of milk and champagne—boring versus special. And they think this will sell?' Noah asked, reading off the results of the final test and preparing to leave the lab.

'Market research says it will,' Jena told him, then she chuckled. 'Though I've no idea who they get to answer questions for research. Probably the same people who answer the ratings questions.'

Noah found himself smiling.

'Showing contempt for the industry that pays your wages, Jena?' he asked, as she followed him out of the room.

'Merely dealing with reality!' she retorted, and this time he was the one who chuckled.

'What's going to happen to Minnie now?' she asked, and the conversational shift took him by surprise. For a moment there he'd almost forgotten his patient.

'I'll start drug treatment and keep fluids running into her, watch her closely and hope for the best.'

'That last bit doesn't sound very professional,' Jena told him.

He grinned at her again.

'No, but we all do it!'

She nodded, then walked away, out into the hall and on up the stairs. Disappointment jarred like a wrong note in a music recital.

CHAPTER ELEVEN

WITH Minnie settled as comfortably as possible, Noah remembered his boast about getting a shower connected up at Matt's place and phoned the plumber who was working on his aunt's house.

'I'm done here,' the man told him. 'In fact, I think Fred has the council inspector coming this afternoon, and as soon as he's given the OK, the kids can move in.'

And I can come back to town, thus avoiding the maddening yet enticing distraction of living with Jena Carpenter.

He wasn't sure whether to feel glad or sad about that, so told the plumber what he wanted and received an assurance that a small tank could be delivered, filled from a water tanker and a hand-held shower installed, all by six at the latest.

'Today?' Noah asked, incredulous at the speed with which the man was willing to organise things. 'In the city I'd have to wait at least a week for someone to look at it, then another couple of weeks for the job to be done.'

'For you, Doc,' the man said, 'I'd put off other jobs—not that I happen to have one this afternoon. The town's real pleased you came. Town this size needs a hospital where folk can go local rather than travelling to the city every time.'

Noah thanked him and hung up, pleased to have his own feelings about the survival of fully functional country hospitals confirmed. Then he smiled in anticipation of Jena's reaction to a fully functional, if cold, shower installed before they reached home.

Home?

The word threw up connotations he didn't want to consider, so he dwelt instead, for a few indulgent minutes, on the smile of delight with which Jena would undoubtedly reward him.

* * *

142

'It's a what?' she shrieked when, in reply to a question about the sudden appearance of a green tank on Matt's back verandah, he mentioned the shower.

'Actually, the green thing's a tank—the shower's inside, in the little bathroom.' After waiting in vain for the smile, he added, 'I thought you'd like it.'

Still no smile.

'I did tell you I'd fix it up.'

'But I don't want a shower!' she wailed. 'What's Matt going to think? His immediate reaction will be, "I told you so!" He'll decide I couldn't hack roughing it and there will go my big opportunity.'

She turned to Noah. Definitely no smile. In fact, ferocious might better describe her appearance.

'You'll have to get rid of it!' she stormed. 'Now! Today! What if he came up. It's not likely, but he could. What will happen then? What about my job?'

Noah stared at her, trying desperately to make sense of the conversation. Sure he'd missed some integral part of the plot, he asked, 'How can installing a shower lose you a job?'

She stopped staring with loathing at the tank and spun to face him, the movement releasing more tendrils of hair, which, he'd noticed the previous day, had a tendency to escape her topknot.

'I'm supposed to be proving something, stupid!' she yelled at him. 'Proving I can live rough, that I can manage under adverse conditions. Then first of all you shift in with me, which immediately gets rid of the isolation aspect of living out here, and now you're putting in hot and cold running water. Do you think I'll get that in the desert?'

They were obviously on different wavelengths, Noah decided. Quite possibly on different planets. He seized on the one bit he could handle.

'It's only cold water, not hot. Will that help?'

The scathing look he received suggested it wouldn't so he tried again.

'What desert?'

Another contemptuous glance.

'Any desert!' she snapped, then she threw up her arms in

disgust and heaved herself out of the Jeep, stalking across to the offending tank and circling it like an animal might have circled an intruder into its territory.

He followed more slowly, mentally reviewing the limited information he had acquired but getting no closer to finding a valid reason for her fury.

Or what job would involve not showering in the desert.

Had she mentioned what the show was about? Perhaps it was more 'real-life' television like the recent spate of mock-survival shows! Or perhaps a female version of the challenges Matt Ryan set himself.

Noah peered cautiously around.

Were secret cameras filming his every move?

No, that couldn't be right. Jena would have refused to have him stay and wouldn't have insisted on secrecy.

'Could you explain a little more? I gather living out here in Matt's shack is some kind of test he's set you. Why?'

She turned towards him.

'To prove I could live rough—and not be worried about little things like not having a shower or being alone.'

'And how will anyone know you can do it? Are there cameras? People monitoring you?'

He glanced around again but Jena's huff of disbelief told him he wasn't under surveillance.

'I didn't have to be watched or monitored. It was for my own sake Matt suggested it. So I'd be sure myself...'

She bit her lip, then cautiously admitted, 'I think he wanted to be sure as well. He knew—well, he thought he knew—I'd do the right thing about it and not cheat. It was a matter of honour—that's what makes you being here so bad!'

He realised she was genuinely perturbed by what she saw as her deception, but Noah couldn't think of anything to console her. He tried for a conversational change instead.

'Is it another challenge, this television show?'

'I can't really tell you but, yes, there's a challenge in the concept.'

'And you'll be expected to live alone? In a desert?'

She shrugged but looked uncomfortable.

'A desert, rainforest, deserted island—wherever!'

'To prove what?' Noah persisted.

She looked at him then, and the frown, previously the slightest of puckerings, deepened.

'It's entertainment!' she muttered, but he guessed the question had unsettled her.

'And that's what you want to do? Entertain people by living in crummy isolated places? You must have wanted it badly to put up with Matt's stupid test.'

'It's *not* a stupid test!' she retorted. 'He had to know I could manage on my own.'

'And can you?' Noah demanded, annoyed with her for letting herself be pressured in this way.

'I don't think that's the question,' she snapped, and turned away before he could ask her what was.

Noah followed more slowly, and found himself watching her elegantly swaying walk and the movements of her supple body. He should have stayed in town. Spent the night at a motel.

He'd have been closer to Minnie, although she'd stabilised and the contractions had stopped by the time he'd left the hospital.

She'd stay in for a few days, maybe a week, then he would consider sending her home, though he'd have to ensure supervision of some kind.

He was still thinking about Minnie when Jena reappeared in her swimsuit and the filmy shirt which seemed to emphasise rather than hide the delectable contours of her body.

If his aunt's house had passed the council inspection today, he could shift the young folk into it tomorrow and be back home himself the following day.

Definitely the wisest move, though he still had a moral obligation to keep an eye on Greg and Rose and, no doubt, he'd be concerned about Jena out here on her own.

Or would Matt be here? Despite her protestations, was she still expecting him? And was the urge to 'prove herself' to him to do with a job or becoming his wife?

The thought of Jena married to Matt Ryan made him feel

physically ill, so he set it aside and hurried into the shack. He'd have a swim, but no kissing.

Definitely no kissing.

But not kissing her was harder than kissing her, he decided, because he couldn't stop himself remembering the ones they'd had, replaying them in his mind when he swam near her—near enough to see water beaded on her lower lip, water he wanted to lick away.

'I'll cook dinner,' he suggested, perhaps prompted by thoughts of lips and licking. 'I've some bits and pieces for a pasta sauce. Do you eat pasta?'

She licked the drops of water away herself, a tiny peak of pink tongue flicking out and disappearing so quickly he might have imagined it had the droplets not disappeared.

'Cooking dinner won't make up for installing a tank without my permission,' she told him coldly, 'but, yes, I do eat pasta.'

The torture continued when he returned to the shack—a long time after he'd seen her leave the water—and found her sitting on the verandah, her long legs propped against the rickety railing. She was wearing shorts and a shirt knotted at the front, and her fair hair was trailing wetly down her back.

She was towelling the ends of it, and the urge to take the towel from her hands and help dry the lustrous mass was so strong he didn't dare walk past her but took himself around the back where he stood for a long time under the cold shower, reminding himself of all the reasons he didn't want a relationship.

And, anyway, she was adamant she didn't want one either!

'Did you find what you were looking for in the library?' he asked, joining her on the verandah when his sauce was simmering and he was fairly certain other parts of him weren't. He'd pulled on a shirt but had left his swimming trunks on, knowing he might need a cooling-off swim later.

She turned and lifted one shoulder in an elegant shrug.

'Yes and no,' she said. 'I found a great book but couldn't borrow it because I'm not a permanent resident and don't have a library card.'

She didn't ask, but he heard the question in the air.

'You can have my card. I joined soon after I arrived. I'll give it to you tomorrow.'

'You're being very helpful for someone who doesn't believe in Christmas cheer.'

It was too dark to see the look in her eyes but he guessed it was mostly suspicion.

'I didn't say I didn't believe in Christmas cheer,' he protested, then admitted, 'Actually, I've a reason. I wondered if I could be part of the group you're coaching—go in with the kids for the parade?'

Jena couldn't believe what she was hearing.

'You want to be in the parade? You, the man who thinks the whole thing's ridiculous and Christmas is already far too commercialised?'

'I have my reasons,' he said stiffly, and Jena laughed.

'Someone suggested you be part of the hospital float and you knew there'd be fake noses and had to find an excuse!' she guessed, and saw from a twitching movement of his shoulders that she was right. 'Well, we're rehearsing at six-thirty tomorrow evening if you'd like to come. No doubt you know the way to the house.'

'You're rehearsing to be statues?' he demanded. 'Isn't standing still a prerequisite of being a statue? What's to rehearse?'

Jena chuckled.

'If you want to be part of it, come along and see,' she told him.

'I will,' he promised, but Jena heard reservation in his voice and wondered if he was already regretting the rash suggestion.

Although painting Noah Blacklock's finely moulded body with silver or gold body paint might be rather fun.

Or very dangerous!

He excused himself to serve dinner, and by the time he returned she had her imagination back under control.

'How are you finding life in a small town?' she asked, when she'd taken the edge off her hunger and praised the meal he'd produced, given the limitations of only one gas ring.

'Interesting,' he replied. 'Although my grandparents—my mother's parents—lived here so I visited often as a child, and we holidayed by the lake every Christmas, so I knew the town quite well.'

He'd leaned forward as he'd answered and the lamplight caught a gleam of something she couldn't identify in his eyes. Surely not a smile?

Perhaps a nostalgic one.

'Is it all you hoped it would be?' she asked.

Noah did smile now, though not with nostalgia.

'We're back to "Jena, don't go on and on", aren't we?' he teased. 'Having left half a dozen of your questions unanswered this morning, you're now steering me back towards them.'

'What questions?' She had to think, because she'd started asking questions this time to divert her thoughts from how he looked in the lamplight and how comfortable sitting eating with him was. 'Oh, about the house, the young people? Yes, I want to know that as well, but let's stay with life in Kareela. Is it what you expected?'

He glanced across the table at her and she again saw the lamplight sparkling in his eyes. A twinkle of amusement?

Fun?

'So far I've lurched from one disaster to the next,' he said. 'First Lucy's rejection, then fighting for the halfway house to be set up, arriving here to find a doctor was the last thing Jeff Finch wanted in "his" hospital. To be honest, I thought Linda might have been able to help me sort it out, but—'

'Instead, it warned you of the dangers of drifting into what could even remotely be considered a relationship,' Jena teased.

He sighed, but it wasn't the usual pained sigh he often used when she was around.

'I guess,' he admitted, and looked out towards the lake.

She knew the twinkle would have disappeared, and regretted her remark. In the dusky night air she felt attuned to the man and could sense a battle raging beneath his skin.

Not that she didn't have troubles of her own beneath her outer covering. It was as if a sense of him had coiled its way into her being, twining around her heart and lungs, so glimpses of twinkling eyes and lurking smiles were greeted with an inner tightening.

'Tell me about the halfway house,' she suggested, as her thoughts veered dangerously towards considerations of attraction. 'You said Lucy thought you were mad, giving away your city house, so obviously you haven't been involved with drug rehabilitation for a long time or she'd have accepted, if not expected, it.'

This time the sigh was different, merely a flutter of escaping air from lips which had featured vividly in her dreams. When he spoke, Jena felt it was a story he'd been more than ready to tell.

'The single motivating factor was a thirteen-year-old girl I couldn't save.'

The words shocked Jena, wrenching at the coils inside her, and for a moment she regretted her questions. But the sense that Noah needed to talk remained. Maybe some of his anger was a result of bottling up too much of his emotional reaction.

'Thirteen is too young to die,' she said quietly, not wanting to prompt more revelations, or cut them off.

'Far too young,' he agreed. 'It made my inability to save her so much worse.'

She heard heartache as well as deep regret in the words and felt remorse at having teased him for not having 'fun'. How petty it must have sounded.

'I'm sure no one expects doctors to be able to save everyone,' she protested.

'No one except the doctor himself.'

The words lingered momentarily, but Jena couldn't let it rest. Not when he was hurting with the memory.

'That's ridiculous!' she said. 'And insane! No one could work effectively with such a huge load of self-expectation. You must have known before you even started studying that doctors aren't invincible, that they can't alter fate or totally defeat death.'

Noah found himself smiling at her passion. He could remember feeling it himself—once upon a time!

'No, I had no God-like concept of my own or my colleagues' infallibility, but Amy was a youngster I felt I should have saved. She'd been in before when she'd taken some poor-quality drug, and she'd talked about going into a rehab programme, then suddenly she was there again. I tried everything I knew, but she was too far gone. It was as if her heart didn't want to keep beating—as if it had no reason to battle on.'

He looked across at Jena, and told her something he'd only previously acknowledged to himself.

'It was the waste that got to me. A life thrown away like last week's flowers. She was still a child, but one who'd had no chance to know real childhood.'

He felt pressure on his fingers and realised Jena had taken his hand, so he told her what he knew of Amy's story and saw tears slide down his listener's cheeks.

'She had a lottery ticket in her hand the last time,' he explained, now so far into the story he couldn't stop. 'She gave it to me before she died. It won a lot of money.'

The words dried up, but Jena had followed closely, apparently in her heart as well as in her mind, for she leapt to what he'd felt had been the only conclusion.

'You spent it on the rehab place in Brisbane. To help other Amys.'

'A lot of them don't want to be helped,' he said, absurdly pleased by her guess. 'And others find the going far too tough. But for those who make it through the programme, we needed somewhere for them to begin to put their lives back together.'

She'd released his hand, and now sat back.

'But did you need to be involved in that part of it?' she asked. 'Did you feel you had to give up your job and come up here to supervise things? And why Kareela? Couldn't you have stayed involved in the programme in Brisbane? Given time there if you wanted a hands-on input? '

She was going on and on again, but he didn't find it irritating. In fact, her questions were forcing him to think through what might have been gut decisions—though Lucy and many of his friends had described them less charitably. And even without Jena's hand in his, he felt connected to her somehow.

'I didn't and don't need to be involved at all—in fact, I'm

not. As far as the programme in Brisbane is concerned, the money from the lottery win went into a trust and income from the trust pays professional staff. Getting people off drugs is way beyond my capabilities—and patience, too, I suspect.'

'But Kareela? The house here?'

'Did anyone ever tell you you'd make a good interrogator?' he asked, then he answered anyway. 'I had another house in Brisbane, which I was in the process of selling and which netted me more than enough to buy in Kareela, for all the foolish reasons I've already explained. So letting the rehab people have the old student house wasn't any great sacrifice.'

He hesitated.

'It's hard to remember what happened when, because so many changes occurred in a short time. No, I didn't need to be here from the point of view of involvement with the programme, but experience suggests that people using halfway houses are still very vulnerable. They're still in touch with their counsellors, of course, but if we'd sited it in another town, we could just as easily have found a local who'd be willing to act as a...

How to describe what he perceived to be his role.

'A listener, really! Someone available to talk to when the going gets tough. It's a non-judgmental kind of role. Then my aunt left me the house and it all fell into place. Later, the money from the television programme came in handy to set up a maintenance fund for the Kareela house.'

'Somewhere along the track you must have mentioned some of this to Lucy,' Jena murmured, shaking her head as if the scenario still had massive gaps. 'She must have had some clue as to what was going on!'

The movement made her hair move around her shoulders, shimmering like spun silver in the lamplight. He didn't want to talk about Lucy—or about the past. Not any more. Though talking was better than thinking the kind of thoughts now rampant in his head.

'She knew about the trust and the old house in Brisbane—'

'And understood?'

'Of course!' Noah snapped, more out of loyalty than truth,

for Lucy had given him all kinds of grief over what she'd seen as his foolish generosity. 'The rest of it, the halfway house, came later. When we'd already decided to separate.'

'For a year,' Jena reminded him. 'When, should she want to, she'll tug your string and you'll go running back.'

'It's not that way at all,' he said, angry because she'd spoiled a mood so pleasant it had wrapped around him like an old jacket on a cool night. 'We both needed time apart to work out how we felt about each other.'

The companion he'd thought so empathetic gave a loud snort of derision.

'Surely you're intelligent enough to realise how stupid that sounds! If you really cared about each other, wouldn't a minute apart be too long, a day endless, a week unbearable? And who's going to crack? Are you going to give up your view that the country's a better place to raise children? Or is she going to decide a great house in Kareela is better than a city-hospital career?'

'You can talk!' Noah snorted, though the words made far too much sense. 'What's your life goal? To go traipsing off through bush and desert, proving beautiful women can be as game as any man?'

Lamplight did little to diminish the glare Jena shot at him, but she recovered quickly.

'It's hardly a life goal, simply a job I'd like to tackle, thank you very much!'

She smiled sweetly, added something about him having cooked so it was only fair she did the dishes, then she stacked the plates, lifted them and glided away, leaving an emptiness he couldn't understand.

In the end, he followed, carrying the lamp and setting it down on the bench then turning off the battery light she'd been using.

Tiny bumps of awareness rose on Jena's skin and she pressed against the bench, willing the pot of water she'd put on the stove to boil. Then she felt his fingers touch her hair, his voice murmur, 'It's still a bit damp. Will it tangle if it doesn't dry before you go to bed?'

Such a practical conversation, such a sensible question, so why did the tendrils around her heart tighten painfully, and why was every nerve in her body aching to turn into his arms?

'I'll plait it and tomorrow it'll be all crinkly,' she managed to reply, though her mouth was dry with desire and the crinkly hair the last thing on her mind.

'I could plait it for you,' he offered, his hand now lifting the strands, so close behind her the skin on her neck quivered in expectation of his touch. 'Or rub it, help you dry it off.'

Jena closed her eyes, wondering how much more she could stand. They were talking about her hair, yet her body was responding as if his words were the ultimate in verbal foreplay.

'Tangles in my hair I can handle,' she told him, her voice wobbling with the effort to sound calm. 'It's tangles in my life I've doubts about.'

'Me, too,' he murmured, but he kissed her anyway, right on the back of her neck where the already sensitised skin burned to his touch.

She turned into his arms, felt him reach out to turn off the gas, then met his lips in a kiss that had been so long anticipated she shuddered with the relief of it.

'I don't want to get involved,' he reminded her, breathlessly, a little later.

She kissed the words away, although when once again the exploration left lips to savour skin she did manage a slightly shaky, 'Nor do I.'

Then suddenly she was peeling off his shirt, while his fingers fumbled with her bra catch.

'Could we look on it as a one-night stand?' he asked, now standing in front of her and reverently stroking her breasts.

The ache between her thighs suggested one night might not be enough, but she nodded anyway.

'Or maybe two,' she amended. 'A brief affair.'

He'd stepped back a little so she saw him smile, then he touched her face.

'So beautiful,' he murmured.

She sensed he was prolonging the moment before they ventured further, raising the excitement in both their bodies to a feverish intensity. She lifted her own hands, and ran her thumbs across the hard ridges of his cheekbones.

'You're not so bad yourself,' she whispered back, then let her hands trail downwards, along his jaw, lingering on his shoulders, flitting past nipples already ridged and hard, resting on his belly, her little finger teasing at the indentation.

'Dangerous ground, lady, if you don't want to take it further,' he warned, the words a husky growl which added more fuel to her inner heat.

'Who's seducing who here?' she demanded, smiling at the excitement even words could generate between them.

Her fingers slid lower, thumbs hooking inside the waistline of his bathing trunks.

'There's not even a decent bed!' he grumbled, but the hands that now held her breasts were trembling, and his thumbs teasing gently at her nipples were creating an agony of desire so strong she could barely breathe, let alone respond with words.

She leaned into him, crossing the distance and pressing her aching breasts against his chest, trapping his hands.

'One-night stand!' She confirmed his words, breathing them against his lips, while her hands clung to his shoulders, only will and his strength keeping her upright now.

Noah held her close, as if letting her go would somehow break the spell, yet managed to make a bed for them, using his swag and her thin foam mattress. Then their clothes were grappled off and the urgency they'd held at bay for so long forced the pace. Tangled limbs and murmurs of desire, questions and confirmations, exploration of what worked and didn't, escalating the tension until it reached a cataclysmic release which left them trembling in each other's arms.

Jena let him hold her, revelling in his strength, slowly feeling something like normality seeping back into her body. As the silence lengthened, doubts sneaked in—ecstasy giving way to confusion as to what might happen next.

But no regrets, she realised, searching through what she thought of as her soul. Not a one.

Awkwardness, though.

Trepidation.

A tiny smidgen of panic.

She eased herself a little away from him and looked into what she could see of his face.

'Well, that was fun,' she said, hoping words would ease the strain.

'Fun?' he echoed. 'That's all?'

He ran his fingers lightly down her arm, then slid them across the soft skin on the top of her breast, avoiding an already puckering nipple but alerting senses she'd thought would lie dormant through exhaustion for at least a couple of hours.

Then slowly and meticulously he aroused her again, her growing excitement feeding his own need until she was in no doubt as to his intentions.

Yet again he held back, tormenting her with his sensual teasing touches until she had to bite back the whimper of want which kept trembling on her lips.

'Still fun,' he murmured, moving to lie almost on top of her but with his weight still supported on his side. 'Show me how much fun it is. Touch me and tell me, blonde witch that you are!'

This time their lovemaking was slow, and deep, and consciously prolonged—so exhausting that Jena's toes had barely stopped tingling, the tremors of orgasm barely stilled, when she felt sleep dragging her deep into its clutches.

She woke to birdsong, and a warm body curled around her back. Sensed he was awake, and lying still so as not to wake her.

She snuggled closer.

'Asking for trouble, lady,' he grumbled. 'We're already way behind in our going-to-work preparations.'

She eased herself as far away as his grip would allow, but couldn't bring herself to break the final contact.

'My aunt's house is finished. I could shift the kids and go back to town today.' Sadness gathered in her heart as she read 'goodbye' in the sombrely spoken final words.

'And I should be here on my own,' she told him, agreeing

to what he hadn't said, 'if I'm to honestly fulfil Matt's trial run.'

His grasp tightened, strong arms folding her body into his.

'It was a great night, Blondie,' he whispered.

'And fun,' she reminded him.

Then she eased right away this time, standing up and hurrying towards the back verandah, glad about the shower although she knew darned well the cold water wouldn't be enough to wash away the memories of the night.

Or anaesthetise the ache in her heart.

For a man she barely knew?

Get real here, Jena! she scolded herself.

CHAPTER TWELVE

NOAH had disappeared when Jena, wrapped in a towel because she'd neglected to take clothes with her, came tentatively back into the room. A quick look through the door told her the Jeep was still there so he was probably swimming.

She dressed quickly, though suspecting an armour of clothes would be little protection if they were foolish enough to kiss again. Then, because she'd already decided to go to the laundromat at lunchtime today, she picked up the scattered articles of clothing off the floor and dropped them into her laundry bag.

Noah returned as she was staring at the plate of breakfast cereal she usually enjoyed. He was in swimming trunks and a shirt, but the trunks were dry.

'I jogged down to check on Greg and his family,' he explained, gathering up a selection of clean clothes as he spoke then disappearing towards the shower.

Jena stared at the empty doorway. If this taut politeness continued, she'd be glad he was shifting back to town—though whether she'd survive this morning's drive without tearing out her hair was another matter.

'It was a one-night thing, you both agreed,' she reminded herself, then she poured milk on her cereal, walked out to the front deck and threw the soggy flakes out for the birds to eat later.

She made herself a cup of coffee instead and, as she carried it out onto the deck, wished she'd taken up smoking as she was reasonably certain this was one of those occasions where a cigarette would have helped.

Or sublimation! Think of something else.

She went back inside, dug through her handbag for her notebook, a pen and her glasses, then returned to the verandah. She'd start on a summary of a typical day at Kareela Hospital, something the director could use to get a handle on the shots he'd want.

She settled into one of Noah's chairs, slipped off her sandals and propped her feet on the railing, and began to write.

She's got those darned glasses on again! Noah realised, as he came back, fully dressed, into the main room of the shack.

He watched her for a moment, then shook his head. Even if he wasn't off relationships, which he was, she didn't want him anyway.

Didn't want *any* entanglement.

Somehow the broader concept failed to stop the unsettled feeling in his stomach. Though it might just have been hunger.

Even as he offered the limp explanation to himself, he knew it wasn't true. Hunger didn't manifest itself in tension and a kind of faltering in his pulse when he glanced her way.

He ate some cereal anyway, just in case it might help, but breakfasted propped against the bench inside rather than risk further confusion on the deck.

'Ready in two minutes?' he asked, when he'd put off the moment they would both have to get in the same vehicle as long as he possibly could.

'Be right there,' she assured him, and he saw her ease gracefully to her feet, removing the black-rimmed glasses at the same time and pushing her hair back with one hand.

Then, after slipping glasses, pen and notebook into her capacious handbag, she leant forward and flicked her hands somehow through the mass of hair, twisting it into a knot on the top of her head, and miraculously securing it there.

Except for the silvery strands that escaped and flirted around her face!

As she came back into the room he realised he'd wasted the entire two minutes, so now had to grab his swag and roll it hurriedly into a fat sausage shape.

'I told Greg I'd be back on Saturday to see them. OK if I collect my stuff then?'

He was bent over, trying to do up the swag's straps with fingers that were about as useful as bananas, when he heard a noise he took as assent. Then her feet walked through his field of vision and tap-tapped their way cautiously down the steps.

By the time Noah reached the car he was more composed, or so he thought until he saw what she was wearing. Skin-tight trousers ending just below her knees, revealing swelling calves that just last night had been locked around his back.

He coughed back a betraying gasp, and pressed his palm against his chest in an effort to slow his heart rate.

'If I could get the library card when we get to the hospital, I'll go down and see what books there are. I'd like to have something to think about during the day.'

Something to think about during the day? He wanted to shriek the bland phrase right back at her. Hadn't last night meant anything? Given her any kind of thrill that just might possibly have lingered in her mind?

For an hour or two, at least?

Feeling very hard done by, he muttered agreement and concentrated fiercely on the road. Getting her away from the environs of the hospital to the library was undoubtedly a good idea, considering the way his body was reacting to her presence in the car.

After what seemed an interminable drive, he finally pulled up in the parking lot, felt in his hip pocket for his wallet to find the library card and realised that in his haste he must have left it at the shack.

'Rhoda will lend you a library card,' he said, refusing to confess his stupidity. He'd find time to whip back out later. The place was unlockable but vandalism in the isolated area was so rare his wallet would be safe.

Jena wondered why Noah's library card was suddenly not available to her, but as the questions she'd ventured to ask on the tense drive in had been answered in terse one- or two-word sentences, she decided not to mention it.

'Not only will I lend you my library card,' Rhoda told her, 'but I'll give you some money from petty cash. Would you mind calling at Davidson's and picking up some Christmas decorations for the wards? I went through the old stuff we have here and by the looks of it mice have been nesting there for the last twelve months. Most of it's fit only for the rubbish bin.'

After checking that the mock-up of the office and theatre were proceeding upstairs, Jena went out to the car park, collected her laundry bag from Noah's car, dropped it into her own, then hopefully started the engine.

It fired first time and, after a thankful pat to the dashboard, she set off. Laundromat first to throw the clothes in a machine, then library, then shops. Her conscience suggested she should really be at the hospital, perhaps following the yardsman or domestics around, but being there meant being close to Noah, and right now she needed distance.

And some time to answer a few questions of her own—like why she *wasn't* feeling guilty about sloping off work when usually her work ethic was close to perfect.

Because the work she was doing no longer seemed important?

Surely that couldn't be the case.

When she'd first switched to working in television, she'd found it challenging and satisfying, while coming to Kareela had been like pausing in an open doorway with the whole world stretched before her, the prospects limitless.

So why did that world now look less glittering?

Less appealing?

She sighed as she pulled up outside the laundromat. Davidson's was two doors down, the library in the next street. She'd start the wash, walk over there…

Noah returned to the men's ward after lunch. He'd begun the day with a phone call to the council inspector who'd assured him his young friends could move into the house. Given the work schedules of vegetable-pickers, it had been too late to organise the house shifting today, so he'd decided he could camp in his aunt's house himself for a couple of nights and have the kids move in over the weekend.

Certain he'd delayed long enough for Jena to have left the premises, he'd then done a ward round, sending Toby home, recommending physio for Colin and promising Mrs Burns she'd be out before the weekend. After checking Minnie, who'd been stable, the contractions gone, he'd settled in his office and tackled his paperwork.

At midday, as a reward for a job well-done, he'd taken himself back out to the lake, where he'd retrieved not only his wallet but, conscious of the dangers of returning when Jena was there, his swag, clothes and toilet gear. He'd considered leaving his small refrigerator and food supplies, then had smiled to himself as he'd remembered Miss Independent's fury over the shower.

Best he take them, too, he'd decided, if he didn't want her yelling at him again. Though yelling had been better than the polite attempts at conversation she'd made earlier this morning, peppering the drive to town with remarks and questions, forcing him to respond when all he'd wanted to do had been to run his tongue across her skin—every inch of it—to taste her sweetness one last time.

Regret that he hadn't achieved this aim clung like a film to his skin, and permeated his mind, making normal thought processes difficult. So to find Jena right in front of him, perched atop a ladder as she nailed one end of a red and green garland to the wall above the door, was an exacerbating experience.

'What are you doing?' he demanded, and she had the hide to grin down at him.

'Want to guess?' she teased. 'What about multiple choice? Am I fixing my hair, taking a shower, cooking dinner or putting up Christmas decorations?'

Colin Craig, who, Noah noticed belatedly, had parked his wheelchair at the foot of the ladder and had a box of decorations balanced on his plastered limbs, chuckled at the joke.

Noah ignored him—and her—crossing the room to speak to the patient he'd come to see. Behind him, he could hear her talking and joking with Colin, and he had to restrain himself from telling her to concentrate on what she was doing—to be careful—not to fall.

In fact, lifting her down off the ladder would be his most favoured option. Then, once he had her in his arms—

He hauled his mind back into medical mode, decided to visit

the other patients later and walked out, detouring through the women's ward so he didn't have to pass Jena again.

'Aren't you even going to comment?' Jill asked. He glanced around and realised this room had already been decorated, gold and silver foil circling the walls like a patterned border, while convoluted red and green streamers spread out from above the fan in the centre of the ceiling to the walls.

'We're putting up a tree as well, in the hall,' Jill told him. 'It's the old one we've had for ages. Apparently the mice didn't like the taste of that particular plastic.'

The explanation made no sense whatsoever to Noah but, then, nothing much did today. He headed back to his office where a proposal to set up a hospice in the area needed his attention.

Or what attention he was able to give it.

Jena's ancient LandCruiser was gone from the car park when he finally left work, but the note under his windscreen wiper started his nerves jumping again.

'Meeting tonight at your house if you want to be part of Carla and co.'s float,' she'd written, her handwriting neatly upright, projecting an image of the bespectacled Jena he didn't want to be seeing in his head.

Indecision kept him rooted to the ground. It was already six-thirty, the designated 'rehearsal' time, so he had to move if he wanted to avoid being part of the 'false noses and giant syringe' frivolity.

Against that, of course, was the added contact with the one woman he wanted to avoid, but how many 'rehearsals' would one need to be a statue?

'Plenty!' Jena said, telling Suzy, who'd actually asked the question, not long after Noah had arrived and taken a seat on the back verandah of his own home.

Jena was propped against the outdoor table, her long legs crossed at the ankle—the very picture of a woman totally at ease. He studied her as unobtrusively as possible, unable to believe she could be as relaxed as she appeared when he was strung tighter than a pro's tennis racket.

'Why?' Davo asked.

'Because I think it will work better. I'll show you. Come on, Carla, and Suzy, and you, too, Will. Stand up here and be statues. Carla, you're like this.' Jena stretched out her arms as if holding a bow with an arrow fitted to its string. 'Suzy, like this.'

This time she made out she was holding a shallow bowl, her slim arms curled gracefully out in front of her, fingers making the pose look—well, statuesque!

Will she positioned like a man delivering a speech, one arm outstretched as he gestured to his audience. When she had the three posed to her satisfaction, in a loosely structured circle, she whispered to each in turn then went back to join the 'audience'.

When the stillness of the three had gone on so long Noah wondered if Jena had hypnotized them, she murmured, 'Now!' The poses changed. Each statue took on the position of person to the left of him or her.

The stillness reigned again, so complete that Noah wondered if he'd imagined any of the three had ever held a different pose.

'OK, relax,' Jena told them, then she appealed to all the group. 'What do you think? Don't you think the pose changing, preferably right down a line, would make it so much more interesting?'

The young folk all agreed with her, as did Noah, though he didn't feel obliged to add his voice. After all, Jena was treating him as just another member of the group—and he could be offhand, too, if he tried.

She opened the books she must have chosen from the library, showing pictures of statues which had what might be considered typical poses. The young folk tried them out, then fooled around a bit, pushing at each other, but fell quiet when Jena spoke again.

'It's not easy,' she reminded them, 'and has to be perfectly done to be effective. No one's going to be impressed by a statue who's shuffling his or her feet, or scratching body paint from his nose. I've spoken to our carpenters and they'll rig up a float fitted to the back of my vehicle. It will be a simple stage with a circle of light cardboard columns on it, and you'll pose between them.'

She flipped through the book to where another picture illustrated the general idea of a small temple to the gods.

'Could you leave the books?' Suzy asked.

'And come back again early next week to see how we're going?' Will added. 'After all, the parade's Saturday fortnight. Not far away.'

Jena agreed, talked some more, then said she'd have to go.

'Stay to dinner,' Carla suggested, but Jena shook her head.

'I'd rather get home,' she replied.

'Since no one's invited me to stay to dinner, I'd best be going, too,' Noah said, immediately prompting warm invitations from his young friends.

He raised his hands and smiled.

'I was teasing! I've got to go back up to the hospital for a while.'

'Thanks for coming,' Davo said, then he looked embarrassed but added gamely, 'For everything. This house, the programme, helping out. We know you hate us saying we're grateful, but we truly are.'

Jena watched Noah cope with his own embarrassment. He wasn't a man who found praise easy to accept. Found anything easy to accept, she guessed.

'Are you sure you're going to be all right out there on your own?' he asked, catching up with her as she walked around the side of the house towards her car.

'I'll be fine,' she assured him. Truthfully, as it happened, because she was certain she'd feel better once she got away from him—from the temptation to touch him, kiss him, beg him for one more night together.

No! No begging, Jena, she reprimanded herself, and missed what he was saying.

'I'm sorry. My thoughts were miles away,' she said—not true that time. 'What were you saying?'

'I wondered if you'd like to have dinner with me. By the time you drive out to the lake and cook something yourself it will be very late.'

Have dinner with him? Sit across a table from him again? Watch the way his hands held cutlery, his lips moved as he ate?

'No, thank you,' she said politely, though desire warred with common sense and she knew if he pushed she'd probably weaken.

'You're probably right,' he admitted, but though they'd reached her car he didn't move away.

'I've told Carla and co. they can have the house until the weekend. I'm staying at my aunt's old place until then. Do you want to see it?'

She looked him in the eyes, breathed deeply and said, 'I thought we'd both agreed it was a one-night stand.'

Saw a smile stretch one corner of his lips.

'And if we're together in a less public place than this we'll lose all control? Is that what you're saying?'

She returned his smile, although her heart was thudding heavily with a mix of loss and desire.

'It's more than likely, isn't it?'

He touched her then. Just one finger, sliding up her arm.

'Is there such a thing as a two-night stand?'

She'd shivered at the touch, but the words made her feel even colder.

'Not for this chick!' she said, hoping the words sounded flippant enough to cover her own sense of loss. She remembered suggesting the two-night thing the previous night. But spending another night in Noah's arms, making love with him again, would magnify the difficulties she was experiencing, not remove them.

Noah nodded, as if to accept her thoughts as well as her words, but his voice, when he murmured, 'Take care,' was gravelly with more than concern.

It was impossible to avoid Noah at work the following day, as it was minor-surgery day and Jena wanted to see as much of it as possible. This was what they'd use the mock theatre for, and it would be up to the editor to cut shots from the real thing in with long and angled shots which would be taken upstairs.

She'd just have to banish all thoughts of their lovemaking from her mind.

Being crammed into the small theatre with Noah, one of the local GPs who acted as anesthetist, plus two nurses, was hardly conducive to banishing him from her mind, but she got through the day and headed gratefully back to the shack—deciding that the loneliness and the ache his absence generated was better than being near him and aching for his touch.

On Saturday, as she walked along the beach, she met up with Greg and Rose and the two little girls. Jena played with the children, building a sandcastle complete with turrets and a moat while their parents swam.

Tired of the sandcastles game, they turned on her for amusement, indicating with signs and little pushes that she lie down. They began to shovel sand over her, so intent on their task she was able to close her eyes and think of Noah—of why, on so short an acquaintance, she found him so appealing.

Because he'd made it very obvious he wasn't available? Had her subconscious seen it as a challenge?

Trying to answer honestly, she decided it wasn't that. Heavens, she'd said the same thing often enough to have respected his wish to not get involved.

Not that they had got involved. Which was the hard part. Though the man had appeared to be slightly staid at first meeting—well, angry at first meeting but coming across as staid on further acquaintance—there'd been something about him so attractive, to Jena anyway, that she'd been kissing him on day two!

Not like her at all.

Had the fact that she hadn't wanted to get involved with anyone right now made her reckless?

She was darned if she could think of any other explanation!

Except, of course, the one she refused to contemplate. Love at first sight simply didn't exist. You got to know a man as a person first, and love developed. It didn't come crashing down on you with all the unpredictability of a summer thunderstorm.

She was buried up to her neck, only her face visible, her

brain tossing suggestions about, arguing and discarding but getting no closer to a solution, when two long, bare and very masculine legs appeared in her limited line of sight.

'I know they make glass from sand. Is this a variation of Sleeping Beauty's glass coffin?'

Before Jena could answer, the children were greeting Noah with shy smiles, then dragging him towards the water to swim with them, leaving Jena, encased and forgotten, in the sand.

She broke out quite easily, lifting first one leg, then the other, sitting up and shaking herself. But sand stuck everywhere. It was caked on her body, and thick in her hair.

Great! she thought. A truly glamorous image to present to the man who's haunting your dreams.

She walked slowly down towards the water, wondering if she could swim far enough out to strip off her bikini to wash out the sand that had crept under it.

Then she'd have to put it back on again, which might not be easy while treading water in the middle of the lake.

She was still considering this when she reached the water's edge, some distance from where two excited little girls were splashing around Noah, apparently using his body as a surfboard and clambering all over him. Greg and Rose had finished their swim and were sitting, hand in hand, on the damp sand at the edge of the lake.

Jena waved to them but kept her distance, diving in well away from Noah.

Though distance did little to diminish her physical longings, or ease the muddle in her mind.

She swam parallel to the shore of the lake, towards the part of the beach in front of Matt's shack. She'd left her towel and shirt there and only later had walked along and joined the family. Not saying goodbye was rude, but it couldn't be helped. Surely she deserved a couple of Noah-free days a week.

He didn't call in later, although, knowing he was out at the lake, she'd both hoped and dreaded he would. Neither did she see him on Sunday, so by Monday she was so uptight she'd decided that seeing him was better than not seeing him, despite the different kind of anguish contact with him entailed. She drove to work early so everything would be in readiness for the rest of the crew.

Clint Miles, who would narrate the series, was already there, chatting to Linda Carthew in the foyer as Jena came through from the back. One glance at the pair suggested that maybe Linda had found someone to console her after Noah's intransigence.

'Sweetheart!'

Clint greeted Jena with a bear-hug just as Noah appeared from the reception area. 'You've survived out there in the wilderness? I couldn't believe it when Matt said he'd set such a stupid test. He showed me the place once. It's a wreck.'

Jena, used to his theatrics, simply smiled. Surviving life in the shack was a snack compared to surviving the problems in her personal life, which had just been exacerbated by the glimpse she'd had of Noah's face as Clint had hugged her.

The Mr Happy scowl had nothing on the one he was now wearing. She muttered an excuse to Clint and slipped upstairs.

Noah watched her go, and knew she was escaping. He felt like doing it himself, only he couldn't decide whether occasional tantalising glimpses of her were better than nothing at all or if they simply made his inner turbulence worse.

He spoke politely to the man Linda introduced, though he wondered how Jena could put up with the false heartiness which seemed to infect theatrical people.

Sour grapes, mate! he warned himself, but warnings had ceased to work.

Excusing himself, he headed for the wards, but apparently there was to be no escape.

'You can't start a ward round until the cameraman gets here,' Rhoda told him, introducing him to Rod and offering the further information that he was the director and he'd be working from Jena's notes, which apparently she'd emailed him on Friday, to tell the cameraman what shots to take.

'Jena's warned us to be as unobtrusive as possible and, while you must think that's impossible, we'll only use one camera to follow you through your daily routine, though we'll have two set up in the mock office and theatre.'

Noah nodded as if he actually understood what the man was talking about, but as Jena reappeared at that moment, followed by a young chap carrying a camera the size of a suitcase, he stopped pretending to understand and concentrated on not touching her.

'Ward round,' Rhoda suggested helpfully. 'We can start now.'

Noah glanced around, desperate to connect to reality once again. Not that glancing around helped much. Now that he looked at them, he realised all his female patients were decked out in new nightdresses or pyjamas, ranging from classy through glamorous to fun cartoon nightshirts.

'Well, you could hardly expect them to be filmed in hospital issue, could you?' He heard the whisper and knew it was Jena. Hoped she couldn't read *all* the thoughts he was having!

Somehow he got through the day, though his patience had worn very thin by lunchtime. So at four-thirty, when he was about to give himself an early mark and sneak off home—to his own home—and someone suggested taking shots of him in the mock office, he snapped a blunt refusal and shut himself in the lab under the pretext of having tests to run.

'We could film you there,' Rod said hopefully.

'You're here for a fortnight,' Noah retorted. 'You'll have more than enough time.'

Rod looked startled, but as Noah shut the door in his face, there wasn't much he could do about it.

Except knock?

More a tap than a knock, but Noah heard it anyway and flung the door wide, intending to say a few choice words to the persistent man.

Only it wasn't a man, it was a woman.

The one woman he didn't want to see.

CHAPTER THIRTEEN

JENA hovered uncertainly on the threshold.

'Can I come in? I don't want to disturb you if you're really working, but if you're only hiding out, I'd like to explain.'

Though her beauty hit Noah like a sledgehammer every time he saw her, this afternoon it was her uncertainty that was affecting him more, squeezing at his heart with a vice-like grip.

He reached out, grabbed her forearm, hauled her through the opening then shut the door behind her.

'Explain what?' he demanded, angry with his weakness where this woman was concerned.

'About the pressure the crew is putting on you. With Christmas so close, they're hoping to finish early—maybe get all the film they need this week, instead of going into next week.'

He should have been relieved. One week of interference instead of two—only one more week of Jena's presence. But the heaviness in his chest denied him relief.

'Their suggestion or yours?' he asked, then, because he couldn't help himself, he reached out and touched one of the tendrils of hair framing her lovely face.

She flinched and he drew back as if she'd bitten him, but she caught the reaction and touched his hand in apology.

'Dangerous stuff, this touching,' she said quietly.

'Very dangerous,' he agreed, but he gave in to the ache in his arms and touched some more, drawing her close against his body and holding her tightly to him.

'I don't suppose you'd reconsider the career move that makes an entanglement impossible?' he murmured, rubbing his cheek against her hair.

'"Entanglement" was your word, "complication" was mine,' she reminded him. 'And you don't want an entanglement, remember.'

'I could change my mind,' he offered.

'Try me out as some kind of test to set against whatever hold Lucy has on you?'

He tightened his grip on her, wondering how a woman he barely knew could home in so unerringly on his weak spots.

'Stupid, isn't it?' he whispered as his body began to get excited about what had begun as—and was meant to be—a purely asexual embrace.

'Totally!' she agreed, but she snuggled closer as if her body, too, needed the balm of tight contact. Then she sighed, and pushed herself away.

'I don't mean you have to do more filming tonight,' she said, reverting to what she'd obviously come to say, 'but I wanted you to know what's in their minds. That they're as eager to be done here as you are to be rid of them. According to Rod, the time was over-estimated deliberately so you wouldn't be put out if it took longer.'

Noah nodded.

'See you tomorrow,' she added, and she turned, opened the door and walked out, the droop of her shoulders suggesting she was as unhappy about leaving him as he was about her departure.

The week passed swiftly. Noah made an excuse to miss statue rehearsal, knowing that seeing even more of Jena with voluntary after-hours involvement would be a torture he couldn't endure. Though he did invite the young people to a barbecue the following evening, so they could show him what to do. No matter how he felt about Jena, he needed to be on the float to avoid the false noses.

'She won't be here if the crew leave early,' he said, when Carla berated him for changing position too early, telling him Jena would rip shreds off him if he did it on the day.

'She's staying on,' Suzy explained. 'Apparently, she's had some bet with her boss that she'll stick out three weeks in the shack at the lake, and has to stay whether they're filming or not. It's good because it means she can shoot down to Brisbane one day and pick up the body paint we'll need.'

Noah took in the words, but didn't think about them, too

busy trying to work out why the thought of Jena's departure—
no, not the thought but actually putting it into words—had
caused him such heartache. Seeing her around the hospital was
torture. He should be glad she was going.

The explanation didn't occur to him until the following week,
when he realised the torture of not seeing Jena far outdid that
of seeing her. He remembered something she'd said when
they'd been talking of Lucy. Something about a minute apart
being too long, a day endless, while a week...

The description of the week had slipped into some blank
spot in his mind but he could supply any number himself.

Agony. Anguish. Devastation.

But Jena had been describing love—or the reactions of
someone *in* love.

Had she felt it herself, that she could describe it so accu-
rately?

He groaned to himself. Even thinking of her in love made
his gut clench, while imagining her unhappy—as wretched as
he was right now—made him want to belt someone.

Anyone!

'The Health Department have asked us to submit a more
detailed proposal of the hospice you were considering.'

Jeff Finch came in on cue but when Noah realised what he
was saying, he forgot about belting him—even lost his usual
urge to fight with the man.

'They're interested?'

Jeff nodded and smiled, all former animosity gone. It didn't
take long for Noah to guess why. Should they get funding for
the hospice, it would be more money for Jeff to administer—
expanding his little empire quite considerably.

'I wouldn't want it at the hospital,' he reminded Jeff, then
added a sop. 'Although, of course, it would still be under your
authority.'

'Could we get together on it soon?' the CEO asked, seeming
pathetically anxious to smooth over past differences.

'This evening would be good,' Noah said. He knew there

was another statue rehearsal but, despite the pain of not seeing Jena, he knew in his heart it was best this way.

'Well, this evening I've promised the television carpenters I'd check out the float. You know the production company agreed for them to stay on after they dismantled the rooms upstairs to help us build it.'

Jena's work, Noah knew. She'd used the hospital float as an excuse to keep the carpenters in town and had them finishing her 'temple' float as well.

One excuse gone. Could he think of another?

No!

Avoiding her be damned. He'd go to rehearsal. He'd let her push his arms into the right positions. Be close to her, and suffer the consequences later.

Only she wasn't there. He arrived at his aunt's house right on time—six-thirty—and found all the others gathered. Suzy insisted they start without Jena, but anxiety burned like acid in Noah's belly. A light rain had been falling most of the afternoon, the kind that turned roads slippery.

'Was today the day she was going to Brisbane?' he asked, thinking she might have been delayed on the journey.

'No, that was yesterday,' Carla—who apparently knew everything—told him. 'She was having a day out at the lake today. The people at your house wanted to go to town and she was babysitting the kids.'

The anxiety tightened. Though he knew Greg was calm now, the earlier incident wouldn't leave his head. In the end he had to excuse himself.

'I'll just drive out and check everything's OK. She had a flat tyre the first day she was here. Hope she had the sense to get it fixed.'

He knew the words sounded weak, but he no longer cared. The thought of Jena in trouble, maybe hurt, had sublimated everything else.

He reached the accident at the same time as his mobile rang, the hospital warning him he'd be needed when the injured were brought in.

It was just before the turn-off to the lake—a bus slewed

across the road, a small car wedged beneath its wheels, another older vehicle on its side some distance away, while beyond that various other vehicles had pulled over on the verge.

It had happened long enough ago for the police to have cleared a lane for traffic to pass, and cars crawled slowly by, the occupants peering fearfully towards ambulances already loading the injured.

Having assured himself that the damaged vehicle wasn't a LandCruiser, Noah parked off the road and crossed to the nearest policeman, a man who presumably was with the highway patrol as he was a stranger to Noah.

'I'm a doctor—what can I do?'

'We've some people still trapped in the bus, and the ambulance crew are working in there. There's a woman in a bad way in the old van. The paramedic set up a drip and there are helicopters on the way to airlift her and the other badly injured to Brisbane. The less injured will go to Kareela.'

As he finished speaking, Noah heard the *whump* of rotor blades announcing the first helicopter's arrival.

He hurried to the bus, anxious to be of help, but the ambulance attendant waved him away.

'We're managing here. Can't do much until we cut away more of the metal then we'll probably need you. Can you check the woman in the van?'

He sensed Jena's presence before he saw her, perhaps smelt the faint familiar fragrance emanating from the soap she used.

'It's Minnie, Noah!' she whispered, her voice husky with tears that were also streaming down her face. 'She's dead.'

Jena was sitting awkwardly in a corner of the upturned van, the slim, lifeless figure of the young woman cradled on her lap.

'When?' he demanded, squatting down beside the young woman and feeling for a pulse.

'Only a few seconds ago, but look!'

Jena lifted a padded dressing from Minnie's chest, revealing a gaping wound suggestive of damage beyond repair.

'She lost the baby, too,' Jena murmured.

While you sat and held her, comforted her, Noah thought.

But he knew he couldn't linger to offer comfort in turn to Jena. Not when other lives might hang in the balance.

'I have to see to others. Shall I help you out of there?'

She shook her head.

'I'll hold her a little longer. It's still drizzling out there. I don't want her to get wet.'

He touched the woman who'd caused such chaos in his life gently on the cheek and walked away.

By the time he reached the bus the first helicopter was being loaded and more passengers had been reached, so first-aid measures were in full swing. Knowing the ambulance officers could handle all the immediate requirements of providing airways, stemming bleeding and starting fluids, he took on the job of triage, sorting priorities. The woman with her leg severed below the knee would go on the next helicopter, already kicking up spray as it landed on the roadway.

The unconscious man with no obvious head injury would be OK in Kareela where they'd watch for any deterioration of his condition. So Noah worked and sorted, acting automatically as his years of experience in emergency medicine asserted itself.

Once the airlift was complete, and other seriously injured passengers sent on by ambulance to the city, Noah knew he'd have to follow the local ambulance back to Kareela, where he'd have the job of patching and setting and stabilising those less badly injured.

Surely someone had taken Minnie away by now? But where was Jena? What would she do? How would she cope with the shock of what she'd been through?

Aware he had no time to lose, he searched hurriedly among those working to clear the road.

'We're off, Doc,' the ambulance attendant called to him.

'I'm right behind you,' he promised, and trod wearily towards his Jeep.

The thought of Jena driving back out to the lake, bloody and alone, tormented him, but he couldn't go to her, any more than he could have spared the time to comfort her earlier. As he worked through the night, ending up with seven more patients than he'd had the previous afternoon, he realised just how much she meant to him.

How much he loved her.

At dawn, with the adrenalin which had kept him going all night fast draining from his system, he showered off the worst of his exhaustion, pulled on clean clothes, grabbed his mobile in case he was needed urgently and headed for the Jeep.

On second thoughts, he wasn't going to be worth anything the way he was feeling so he headed back into the hospital, phoned Tom Jackson and asked him to take any urgent calls until midday.

Back to the Jeep.

Aware of the dangers of driving while tired, he took his time, slowing even more at the scene of the accident, amazed there was so little evidence of the previous evening's carnage.

He eased the Jeep along the track to Matt's shack, which came into view around the last bend.

Where was Jena's LandCruiser? And what was that sporty little 'pretend' four-wheel-drive doing there?

A sourness invaded Noah's stomach, curdling in his intestines. Even before the man stepped onto the verandah, Noah knew it was exactly the kind of 'city' car Matt Ryan would drive.

Jena *had* been waiting for him! *Had* expected him to join her at the shack.

The revelations were so devastating he couldn't move, couldn't put the vehicle into reverse and roar away. Matt was coming down the steps, peering at the Jeep as if trying to ascertain who was in it.

Rage rose up in Noah, a rage so strong it roared in his ears and filmed his eyes with redness. He pushed open the car door, sprang out, hurled himself towards the man who as a boy and teenager had so annoyed him and roared his anger.

'She's not yours, she's mine, and she's better by far than you'd ever know or have the gumption to realise, you sham, you over-inflated ego on legs!'

And with that he did what he should have done years earlier. He punched Matt Ryan solidly on the nose.

It hurt his knuckles far worse than he could have believed, but he had the satisfaction of seeing blood start before he stormed up the stairs in search of the cause of all this trouble.

Who wasn't there, he realised—belatedly.

Far from soothing him, it only raised his blood pressure a bit more.

'Where is she?' he demanded, glowering down at a bemused Matt who was holding a snowy handkerchief to his injured face.

'If you're talking about Jena, I don't know,' he said, the words thick and distorted. He dug in his pocket and pulled out a magazine. 'I came up because I thought she might see this and be upset.'

Totally confused now, Noah took the magazine thrust at him and saw the article was headed by a large picture of Jena, but it was the heading, BIMBOS NEED NOT APPLY, that caught his attention. He felt new anger twisting his stomach as he read 'industry whispers' about a new television show which, according to the idiot reporter, wouldn't be employing people like Jena.

'I can't believe people actually judge others by their looks!' he growled, but he kept the magazine. A photo of Jena was better than nothing. 'And you must be one of them—to make her stay out here as some kind of test.'

Matt moved the handkerchief from his nose and peered at Noah.

'She needed the experience for her own confidence,' he protested thickly. 'So she'd know she could do it!'

He looked as if he wanted to add more, but for Noah the need to find Jena was growing more urgent by the moment. He headed back to the Jeep. She'd been upset. Where would she have gone?

He drove to his place, but Greg and Rose hadn't seen her since the previous afternoon. Back in the car, he looked again at the article, reading beyond the headlines. The reporter mentioned a previous position for which Jena had applied and been turned down, then went on to add statistics about how few models ever made it into the big time in other fields. The implication in the article was clear—models might have the faces and figures to be successful, but on the whole they were, the writer hinted, short on brains.

Seething with indignation on Jena's behalf, Noah drove back to town. Then indignation changed to heart-heavy despair as he thought about attitudes—including his own—and Jena's dogged determination to prove herself. Her constant stream of 'blonde' jokes, he realised, were defensive, pre-empting what people might be thinking. Or what her experience suggested people might think.

He considered returning to the hospital, but knew he had to get some sleep before he could do any effective work. Reluctantly he turned towards his house—which would feel empty and incomplete and would probably never be a home because he'd made such a hash of his life.

He was so tired he walked past the LandCruiser without realising its significance. Jena was asleep on the lounger on the back verandah, curled up on her side, one hand under her cheek.

Maybe the house would become a home after all, he thought, smiling down at her.

Though once she heard he'd punched her boss and, no doubt, lost her all chance of the job she wanted so desperately…

Her eyes opened as if his thoughts had prodded her awake, and the confusion he read in the vivid blueness made him kneel beside her and put his arms around her.

'I didn't want to be alone,' she said, her voice more hesitant than he'd ever heard it.

'You were alone here,' he pointed out. 'I hated having to leave you, not being able to comfort you when you needed it so badly.'

'But you've had to do that so often,' she murmured, moving her hand from beneath her head to rest it against his cheek. 'See people you couldn't save die, and not have anyone to comfort you. And I wasn't alone. I felt you here. Felt you were near, although I knew you weren't.'

Noah heard the words and fancied he heard echoes of unspoken love behind them. He felt a wild irrational hope spring to life in his heart.

Then remembered what he'd done out at the shack.

'I'd have been here earlier, but I looked for you out by the lake—went there first.' He hesitated, not wanting to put his doubts and fears into words, let alone admit his adolescent behaviour.

'Matt Ryan was there!'

Jena sat up with a jerk.

'Matt, out at the lake! Damn! What could he possibly want?'

'To see you,' Noah suggested, as the myriad new feelings he was experiencing jolted him from tenderness back to grouch-mode.

'About the job, I guess,' Jena said, though she didn't sound as excited as she should, considering what she'd been through to 'prove' herself!

Noah tried to think of a way to tell her the next bit, but couldn't come up with anything more than a blunt recitation of the truth.

'I might have wrecked your chance of getting it,' he mumbled, looking into her eyes as his own begged for understanding. 'I punched him.'

The frown she gave him didn't even hint at understanding!

'You punched him? Why on earth would you have punched Matt Ryan?'

'Because he was there,' Noah expounded, but Jena's frown, instead of clearing, deepened.

'You can't go around punching people because they're there,' she told him. 'Was it something from the past? I know the pair of you had a history.'

Now it was Noah's turn to frown, unable to believe the woman couldn't work it out.

'It was nothing to do with the past,' he said crossly. 'It was because he was there—with you. Or I thought he was there with you.'

Now she had the hide to laugh.

'You thought Matt and I—? That he was there with me?'

She held her sides and laughed some more, which was when he realised she was wearing one of his shirts—and because buttons had come undone he knew there was nothing underneath it.

Not now, he told his libido. Got to sort out a few things first.

'Stop laughing,' he snapped, then added, for good measure, 'That's my shirt.'

She stopped laughing, though amusement still lurked in the sparkling depths of her eyes.

'It was on the line. I had to throw away my clothes, then I washed under the tap and borrowed this.'

He wanted to demand it back—right now. To peel it off her body, make love to her for about four days, then maybe rest and start again. But he still wasn't certain where he stood with this love thing—or where Jena stood for that matter.

She watched confusion and doubt chase like leaf shadows across his face, and because, when she'd sat with Minnie and he'd suddenly appeared, touched her cheek and with eyes that had told her all she wanted to know disappeared again, she took pity on him.

She put her finger on his lips so he couldn't blunder into disjointed conversation again, and began. 'For a start, Matt Ryan is not at all interested in me as a woman. In fact, though you must never tell a soul, he's very much in love with his partner Michael. Next, even if he did come to say I had the job, I'm not taking it. I've thought a lot about what you said, about challenges, and I know I need something, well, more real, I guess. I'm not certain what, as yet, but working with people.'

She saw the soft glow of love light his eyes, but still she silenced him, although now her finger was moving over the contour of his lips and she wasn't sure how long either of them would stand the tension.

'Thirdly, we don't know each other very well, and you have a lot of unresolved stuff to get through with your Lucy, but I'm reasonably certain what I want from you is much much more than a one-night stand. Maybe something in the vicinity of a fifty- or sixty-year stand. If that also appeals to you, and you're sure your past is really past, then perhaps we could work together on the future.'

He took her hand and kissed the tip of each finger in turn.

'Are you proposing to me?' he asked, husky-voiced with emotion.

'Merely setting out some ground rules,' she said, then she leaned forward and kissed him on the lips. 'Now, you look as if you've been up all night. How about you get some sleep? I'm going out to see Matt and get some clothes. We missed rehearsal yesterday afternoon, so we'll have to have one to-night.'

He looked at her with something like panic in his eyes.

'But you'll come back? Perhaps stay here? You'd be very welcome.'

She grinned at him.

'How else could we get to know each other?' she teased.

For a week that had started out so badly, it turned into one of sheer bliss. Having Jena in the house brought it to life in a way, he now realised, Lucy never would have. She brought him to life as well, flirting with him, winning laughter from him at the most unexpected times, delighting him in bed, taunting him when out of it, overwhelming him with the love she gave so freely and took so radiantly from him.

'Come on, laziness,' she chided, when he was trying to cling to the remnants of sleep while she trailed her hair along his spine. It was something that, she'd discovered, drove Noah wild, and in the end he turned over to avoid it and grabbed her in his arms.

'No time for this,' she told him firmly, although she nestled closer and pressed little kisses on his neck. 'It's Saturday. Carla and co. will be waiting for us up at the hospital. You've just enough time for breakfast before we get ready for the parade.'

He suggested other forms of breakfast but she was firm, reminding him to wear his swim shorts under his clothes, as that was all she was allowing in the way of clothing for her statues. Draperies would also be used, but after the last couple of rehearsals he'd begun to wonder if he wouldn't have been better taking his chances with the funny noses.

There was something going on. Carla and co. had been giggly at the final rehearsal, and he suspected he was the only one not in on some joke.

Not that much could happen on a parade float.

They met the others in the large car park at the back of the hospital, where the float had been fitted to Jena's vehicle. The hospital float was also having last-minute adjustments. It took two hours for the paint to be applied to Jena's satisfaction, but having her covering his body with it had given him some ideas for future fun.

'Does it have to go in the hair?' he complained as she rubbed the stuff further and further in. It felt grittier against his scalp than it had on other parts of his skin, but as he had been told to keep quiet he daren't ask her why.

'Now, you all remember what you have to do?' she demanded, when they were painted, hair and all, and standing in their initial poses between the pillars.

Everyone made muted noises of assent, having been warned not to move their lips too much in case the paint cracked.

'Great! Now, John's driving and Kate's navigating and she'll call out the change.' So far so good, Noah thought. He'd known John and Kate were returning to Kareela for the parade. In fact, all the crew were here as the hospital float would also be filmed.

'I'll walk beside the float in case there are any problems,' Jena added, then she turned around and picked up a large cage with a white cockatoo inside it.

Where had it come from? And why?

Noah couldn't ask, couldn't even check that was what he'd seen, as the float moved off, going slowly down the street, heading towards the library where they'd fall in with the others before proceeding down the main street.

He couldn't see Jena now, but as they were passing a few people standing outside the hospital gates to get an early view of the float he put Jena, temporarily, out of his mind and concentrated on being a statue.

They'd just reached the bulk of the crowd when a bird landed on his head, and the cries of delight from the onlookers reminded him not to move. He picked out patients he'd treated in the crowd, saw the McDonalds, Greg and Rose both smiling happily as they'd had confirmation of a new job for Greg the previous day. So many people, all clapping and laughing.

But the bird remained.

Maybe at the next change of position, it would go away.

'Shoo!' he muttered, although the word didn't sound too effective through closed lips.

Then it shifted to his shoulder and seemed to be eating something from behind his ear. He glimpsed white feathers and a yellow crest, and several things fell into place.

I'll kill her, he vowed, but the crowd was pointing and applauding and the other statues, though their shoulders were shaking with merriment, were holding their poses well.

The parade ended in the large park near the showgrounds, where the town band was playing Christmas carols. Kate gave the order for them all to relax. The other statues gathered around Noah, all laughing and congratulating each other.

'We got the loudest applause.'

'People loved it.'

'Did you see them clap and point?'

'Jena said it should have been a pigeon but she couldn't get a trained one. It's her brother's cocky and, more than anything else, he loves pumpkin seeds. That's what she put in your hair.'

It was Carla who explained the pertinent details, while Suzy found some spilled seed on the float and, using them, tempted the bird onto her arm.

Noah looked around and saw Jena approaching, the empty cage dangling from her fingers.

Even from that distance, he could read hesitancy in her walk.

As well there might be!

'Did you mind terribly?' Jena asked as she came tentatively to his side.

The people who'd followed the floats were gathering around, showering praise, laughing and joking, still taking merriment from the 'bird on the statue'.

Noah put his arm around her and drew her close, regardless of the body paint spreading liberally all over her clothes.

'No way,' he said, because in retrospect he hadn't. 'In fact, it was fun!'

She turned and kissed him—hard.

'So's most of life,' she whispered. 'But, like love, we just have to work at it, and when we find it, treasure and enjoy it.'

She looked up at him, lips smeared with silver paint.

'We *will* have fun, won't we?'

He nodded solemnly.

'And I worked it out,' he said. 'For fifty years we'd have to call it an eighteen-thousand-two-hundred-and-fifty-night stand, and that's allowing a few nights off for leap years.'

'I think that sounds good,' she whispered, snuggling closer. 'For starters!'

Modern Romance™
...seduction and
passion guaranteed

Tender Romance™
...love affairs that
last a lifetime

Sensual Romance™
...sassy, sexy and
seductive

Blaze
...sultry days and
steamy nights

Medical Romance™
...medical drama on
the pulse

Historical Romance™
...rich, vivid and
passionate

29 new titles every month.

*With all kinds of Romance for
every kind of mood...*

MILLS & BOON®

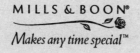

Makes any time special™

MAT4

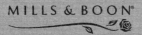

MILLS & BOON®

Medical Romance™

THE MIDWIFE BRIDE *by Janet Ferguson*

With a challenging new job and lovely new home, midwife Ella Fairfax isn't looking for love. At least not until she sets eyes on her handsome neighbour, Patrick Weston! Both single parents with medical careers, they're made for each other. But there is another woman in Patrick's life… is Ella wrong to dream of being his bride?

THE CHILDREN'S DOCTOR *by Joanna Neil*

Paediatrician Anna Somerville knew wealthy, successful heart surgeon Carlos Barrantes was out of her league, despite the sizzling attraction between them. Anyway, she would be leaving the island soon. But Carlos was overwhelmed by his feelings for Anna, and wanted to find a way to make her stay…

EMERGENCY: MOTHER WANTED *by Sarah Morgan*

Casualty officer Keely Thompson is determined to prove to dynamic A&E consultant Zach Jordan that she is no longer the scatty teenager who once declared her love for him. But Zach has also changed —he's now a single father! He and his daughter need Keely's help, but why can't Zach see her in the role of wife and mother?

On sale 4th January 2002

Available at most branches of WH Smith, Tesco, Martins, Borders, Eason, Sainsbury's and most good paperback bookshops. 1201/03b

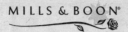

FREE
2 BOOKS
AND A SURPRISE GIFT!

We would like to take this opportunity to thank you for reading this Mills & Boon® book by offering you the chance to take TWO more specially selected titles from the Medical Romance™ series absolutely FREE! We're also making this offer to introduce you to the benefits of the Reader Service™—

* ★ FREE home delivery
* ★ FREE monthly Newsletter
* ★ FREE gifts and competitions
* ★ Exclusive Reader Service discount
* ★ Books available before they're in the shops

Accepting these FREE books and gift places you under no obligation to buy; you may cancel at any time, even after receiving your free shipment. Simply complete your details below and return the entire page to the address below. *You don't even need a stamp!*

YES! Please send me 2 free Medical Romance books and a surprise gift. I understand that unless you hear from me, I will receive 4 superb new titles every month for just £2.49 each, postage and packing free. I am under no obligation to purchase any books and may cancel my subscription at any time. The free books and gift will be mine to keep in any case.

M1ZEC

Ms/Mrs/Miss/Mr ....Initials ....
BLOCK CAPITALS PLEASE

Surname ....

Address ....

....

....Postcode ....

Send this whole page to:
UK: FREEPOST CN81, Croydon, CR9 3WZ
EIRE: PO Box 4546, Kilcock, County Kildare (stamp required)

Offer valid in UK and Eire only and not available to current Reader Service subscribers to this series. We reserve the right to refuse an application and applicants must be aged 18 years or over. Only one application per household. Terms and prices subject to change without notice. Offer expires 30th June 2002. As a result of this application, you may receive offers from other carefully selected companies. If you would prefer not to share in this opportunity please write to The Data Manager at the address above.

Mills & Boon® is a registered trademark owned by Harlequin Mills & Boon Limited.
Medical Romance™ is being used as a trademark.